THE RICHEST FAMILY IN THE WORLD: FAMILY SECRETS

TO: Will

God's best awaits you

E Rogers Sr.

THE RICHEST FAMILY IN THE WORLD: FAMILY SECRETS

Eddie Rogers Sr.

iUniverse, Inc.
New York Lincoln Shanghai

The Richest Family in the World: Family Secrets

Copyright © 2006 by Eddie D. Rogers, Sr.

iUniverse books may be ordered through booksellers or by contacting:

iUniverse
2021 Pine Lake Road, Suite 100
Lincoln, NE 68512
www.iuniverse.com
1-800-Authors (1-800-288-4677)

ISBN-13: 978-0-595-34035-4 (pbk)
ISBN-13: 978-0-595-78823-1 (ebk)
ISBN-10: 0-595-34035-0 (pbk)
ISBN-10: 0-595-78823-8 (ebk)

Printed in the United States of America

<u>Dedication</u>

This story is dedicated to my wife, Delois Rogers, who is the wind beneath my wings.

Special Thanks to Candy Rogers

It was another one of those hot as hell days in the farming communities of south Georgia in the early 1980's. The farms were engulfed in the hot rays of the summer's sun tighter than pigs in a blanket and the heat was threatening to produce another disastrous year for the farmers.

In a cotton field on one of the largest farms in the area, a conversation was taking place between John and Sarah Goodwin, two very frustrated people. They were inspecting the condition of the plants in their fields.

"What do you think, John?" Sarah asked.

"It looks pretty darn bad to me," he replied.

"That's exactly what I was thinking," she said. They looked across the fields and realized all of the plants were in danger of dying. One look at the sky showed them that there was no help in sight. They stood, bewildered, in per-spiration-soaked clothing, in one of several fields that were in desperate need of rain. The heat wave was relentless.

The farmers had been caught in this drought for several years. It seemed like God was punishing the south, but the Goodwins knew this was not the case. It was just part of the risk that they took as farmers. John got down on his knees and dug his large, calloused hands into the ground. Taking some of the soil, he threw it across the field.

"What are you doing?" Sarah asked, watching him.

"The only thing we can do, I asked the Lord to help us. If the weather doesn't change, we're going to lose these crops. If that happens, we'll be on shaky financial ground," he explained to her.

"We have a lot riding on this, don't we?" she asked.

"In reality, princess, we have everything riding on it," John sighed. "If things continue the way they're going, we would have been better off if we had not planted at all this year," he said.

John and Sarah hadn't owed a huge amount of money in the beginning, but it had accumulated over a three-year period because of the drought. Each year they slipped deeper into debt. So far, the bank had extended more credit on their assets to allow them to put in the crops for the following year. Now, they were into their fourth year and the drought was still in full effect. They had tied up all of their assets and didn't have any additional resources available to draw upon. They were at the mercy of the bank and the weather. At present, the weather wasn't cooperating. It would remain to be seen what the bank would do. It was not a good position for farmers to be in, especially during a drought.

"What are we going to do? The bank might not help us again," John asked Sarah.

Wanting to offer whatever comfort she could, she walked over to where he was standing and gently rubbed his broad shoulders. "It's going to be okay," she told him.

The failure rate for farmers had steadily increased. Many of their friends had lost the farms that had been in their families for several generations. Now, the heat wave was putting pressure on the Goodwins who had owned their farm for about 30 years.

Like most of the families in the south, land ownership was very important to them. It had been a wonderful place to raise a family and had been an excellent way for them to acquire wealth. A lot of the work had been done by family members which helped to hold down the cost of labor, but John and Sarah were not the young couple they had been when they bought the farm. They were getting on in years and it was much harder for them to work their way out of these financial situations. Their problems seemed to increase every year.

Before they left their fields for home, John prayed, "Oh, Lord, I try so hard to do the right things. I have always been thankful for the many blessings you have so graciously bestowed on me and my precious family. Oh, Lord, why didn't you send the rain?"

"John, honey, we haven't lost anything. Let's wait and see what the end will be before we jump to conclusions. The Lord will have the final say in this. I know this is stressful and it seems as if it's never going to end, but it will. Now that we're older, these situations carry more weight than when we were younger," Sarah said, remembering their youth. "We believed time was on our side. Now that we're older, we feel the opposite is true. That is one of the reasons that things are more stressful," Sarah said.

"We should have quit four years ago," he said.

"Yes, maybe we should have, but at the time, we didn't know this would happen," she answered.

John and Sarah had been married for 40 years. They were the parents of eight children, five sons and three daughters. They were devout Christians and had instilled their faith in their children. John took pride in the way he and Sarah had raised their family. He had taught them to take pride in being Goodwins.

"Make it stand for something good," he would always say. "As God begins to help you prosper, never get too big for your britches," John advised.

All of their children worked on the farm until they graduated from high school. All eight attended the college of their choice and earned degrees. John and Sarah had stressed to their children to pursue their dreams. John hadn't had that choice when he was growing up. Unfortunately for John and Sarah, none of the children wanted to follow them into the family business.

On their way back home, they talked about the hard work the family had put into the land. John stopped the truck and they walked among the fruit trees that had been put in as seedlings several years ago. So many precious memories were going through their minds as they continued home. When he pulled into the yard, he stopped the truck and Sarah walked over to one of her flower beds. She saw several weeds growing among the flowers and she pulled them out.

John sat in the truck for a few moments and watched how meticulously Sarah attended to her flowers. It reminded him of the days when they first moved onto the farm. She had spent most of her free time working with her flowers. For some reason, it also reminded John of their first encounter.

John met Sarah for the first time at a Saturday afternoon barbeque. She was visiting from Chicago, IL. From the very first sight of Sarah, John was smitten. He couldn't keep his eyes off of her except when she looked his way. She was beautiful. She had been surrounded by a wishful crowd of male admirers when he saw her. Every young man there wanted to talk to her.

John was on the shy side. He lacked self-confidence meeting strangers in social gatherings, especially young, attractive women. He couldn't explain himself like the other young men.

John had never finished high school. Matter of fact, he didn't have very much schooling at all, but he was a handsome young man. Standing 6 ' 2 " tall, he had a neat physique that was chiseled by the hard work he did on his family's farm.

Any time Sarah looked in his direction, he would look away. He didn't think he would have a chance with a young lady as pretty as she was. John couldn't help but be aware of the other young men crowding around her as she sat at the picnic table. He stood near the lake with a friend of his, thinking those guys had it going on. He wished he had the confidence to be seated at the table with her, but he was afraid he would make a fool of himself.

After a while, Sarah got up from the picnic table and started walking in John's direction. John's heart began pounding as she approached him. He turned away and looked out across the lake. She walked up beside him and stopped.

"It sure is pretty and inviting, isn't it?" she asked.

John was so surprised by her presence that his mind went blank. He turned to her like a deer caught in headlights. "What?" he asked.

"The lake, I mean."

"Yes, it's always nice to be around," he replied nervously.

"My name is Sarah, what's yours?"

"It's John, John Goodwin. Where are you from?" he asked, attempting to sound more together.

"I'm from Chicago. Have you ever been there?"

"No, I haven't been there."

"Maybe you'll come for a visit someday," she said as she smiled up at him. "Do I make you nervous?" she asked, noticing his fidgety shuffle.

"Yes, a little," John answered.

"Please don't be. I won't bite you, I promise," she said, teasing him. They both laughed. From that point on, the conversation became a lot easier for John.

John always described the summer he met Sarah as the best he ever had. A lot of people couldn't believe she was attracted to him. They started calling them the odd couple behind their backs.

John didn't have much education and his friends said he probably would be a farmer for the rest of the life. They thought he was a nice guy who was going no where, but Sarah was able to look past all of that and see the real John Goodwin. They both brought joy and happiness to each other's lives.

John's friends were right about John remaining a farmer for the rest of his life, but they were wrong about him not being an achiever. By following God's principles, the Goodwin family eventually became one of the richest families in the world.

"We received a letter from John, Jr. today," Sarah said. There was an instant smile on John's face as he asked, "how's he doing?"

"He's doing just fine," Sarah replied. "He'll be taking a trip home real soon. He wanted to know how we're doing. He's concerned about the drought. He asked how the crops were looking, said he really misses those fishing trips we used to take. He's being considered for a promotion and asks that we remember him in our prayers."

With all of the stress concerning the urgent business at hand, John hadn't taken the time lately to appreciate the blessings the Lord had shared with him and his family. The Lord had blessed them with the fruit of their labor, but just like most people who are going through a difficult time, he was focusing more on what may be lost than what God had blessed his family with. He reminded himself that in all situations, he must continue to praise the Lord.

"Rebecca called today."

There was another smile on his face. John really loved his family.

"She's doing fine also. She said she's having a few problems at her job, but it's nothing that she and the Lord can't handle. She asked me to tell you that she is going to cook you a meal just like the very first one she made for you when she comes home again."

John had some food in his mouth, but couldn't help laughing out loud. "I'll never forget that one," he replied as he began to reminisce on the meal Rebecca has prepared.

REBECCA'S BIRTHDAY DINNER

The first time Rebecca had cooked dinner for him was in celebration of his birthday. She had found the perfect recipes for this special occasion. She asked her mother if she thought she was capable of preparing such a meal. Sarah advised her to plan everything carefully, to get all of her ingredients, and to make sure to follow the recipes exactly as they were written. If she did that, everything would be okay.

Rebecca was so excited. She read and reread the recipes to make sure she knew what to do.

"This is going to be the birthday dinner my father will never forget," she said. "Mother, will you please take me to the market so I can purchase the food items that I'll need?" she asked.

"I'd be glad to," Sarah replied.

When they arrived at the market, Sarah stayed in the car and chatted with friends as they passed by. Rebecca ran inside to get the things she needed. She returned about 30 minutes later with three full bags and eating a candy bar.

"Do you want one, mother?" she asked.

"No thanks, I think I'll save my teeth. I'm going to need them for the rest of my life," she told Rebecca.

"Ah, mother, one is not going to make your teeth fall out of your head," she said, laughing.

"Did you get everything you need?" Sarah asked.

"There were three items I could not find. I'll get them later," she replied.

"Don't forget them," she reminded her.

Rebecca wanted to impress her father on his special day. John had complimented Rebecca about the way she prepared breakfast, but this would be her first full course meal. This was her coming out meal so to speak. After her father's birthday, she wanted to be known as a great cook, just like her mother.

When they arrived home, Rebecca hurried inside and put the items away. Then she went outside to play with her siblings and friends. Rebecca was a straight A student and loved playing softball. When the game finally ended, she came inside and showed her mother the menu.

"What do you think?" she asked. The menu consisted of baked ham, home style green beans, old fashioned mashed potatoes, garden salad, homemade cornbread, and homemade birthday cake.

"Do you know how long it will take you to prepare this meal?" Sarah asked.

"Maybe three or four hours," Rebecca replied.

"Make sure you allow enough time in case something goes wrong," Sarah advised.

"I will, mother," Rebecca answered.

Her father's birthday was two days away. Only family members were invited to the birthday dinner. He always got emotional about the attention he received. This would be especially dear to his heart because his daughter was preparing a full course meal for the first time.

Over the years, Sarah had made sure their daughters spent time helping her prepare the family meals. She had even gotten their sons involved from time to time and encouraged them to learn.

"You might have to cook for yourselves or your families someday," she would say.

May 26th, John Goodwin's birthday, was a beautiful day. The sky was clear and sunny and there was a breeze blowing and it felt really good. John got up early as he did every day. He had breakfast and began his daily chores around the farm. At twelve noon, he came home for lunch. He stayed until one o'clock and went back to work. As usual, Sarah prepared breakfast and lunch. When John finished lunch, she washed the dishes and cleared everything away.

Rebecca was playing with her siblings outside. Sarah went to the front porch and called out to her. She told her she was finished with lunch and that Rebecca could start cooking anytime. Rebecca was wrapped up in a softball game. It was her turn at bat. "Thanks, mom, I'll be there shortly," she called as she moved to the plate.

John and Sarah left the farm to visit his parents' graves. He always cleaned around them and put fresh flowers near their headstones on his and their birthdays. On their way back, they stopped to chat with their friends, Bill and

Emma Herman. They stayed for about an hour and a half talking about the drought and old times.

When John and Sarah got ready to leave, Emma went into another room for a couple of minutes. When she returned, John and Sarah were standing near the truck.

"You forgot something, John," Emma said. John turned in her direction and asked, "What?"

"Happy Birthday!" Bill and Emma exclaimed as they held a beautifully wrapped gift box. John was taken aback. They had never given him anything before. It was a total surprise.

"Did you have anything to do with this?" John asked Sarah.

"No, I didn't," she answered.

"You didn't have to," John told them.

"We know we didn't have to, but we were determined to remember your birthday this year," Emma said. She walked over to John and gave him the gift.

"We were going to bring it over later, but you saved us the trip," Bill said.

"You can still come," Sarah told them. Bill and Emma always brought so much joy with them when they came to visit.

"No, This is your day, John. Share the rest of it with your family," Bill advised.

"Thanks for the gift. By the way, what is it?" John asked, smiling.

"We're not telling," Bill and Emma answered. John and Sarah got back into their truck, laughing. "We'll see you later," they called out.

As John and Sarah yielded at the end of the driveway before turning onto the main road, John unwrapped the gift. Inside, he found a gold pocket watch. "In God's Time" was engraved across the back. Touched by his friends' thoughtfulness, John slipped the watch into his pocket and linked the clip into his jacket. Seeing his expression, Sarah patted his hand.

"I'll pick up a thank you card for them tomorrow," she said as he turned onto the main road and headed home.

When they drove into the driveway of their home, Rebecca was still playing softball. It was around three o'clock in the afternoon. As soon as Rebecca saw them drive into the driveway, she knew she had gotten too involved in the game and had stayed out too long. Sarah wanted to scold Rebecca for forgetting, but John advised her to hold her peace. She followed Rebecca into the kitchen. In a fury of activity, Rebecca started gathering pots and pans. Seeing that Rebecca had forgotten to change her clothes, Sarah reminded her that cleanliness was next to Godliness and pointedly looked at Rebecca's soiled shirt and grass-stained jeans. Rebecca immediately stopped what she was doing and left the kitchen. She went to her room. A few minutes later, she emerged having changed her clothes. She looked tired and seemed to be a little disorganized.

"The kitchen is all yours," Sarah told her as she went back outside to be with John. Rebecca was starting later than she had planned and she was tired. Trying to gather her thoughts, she placed all of her ingredients on the counter. All of a sudden, it dawned on her that there were three items she had never gotten. She decided to cook the ham first since it would take the longest. Both the ham and the cake had to be cooked inside the oven.

'The cornbread, it has to be cooked inside the oven also,' she thought. Time was becoming a major factor. She didn't have enough time to do all three separately so she decided to cook the ham on a higher temperature and put the cornbread in with it. She was going to keep a close eye on the cornbread so it didn't overcook. 'That should do it,' she thought.

She then mixed the ingredients for the birthday cake, poured the batter into the cooking pan, and put the pan into the refrigerator until it was time to go into the oven. She washed the white potatoes and put them on the stove. 'This isn't so hard,' she thought, believing she had gained control and that everything would be okay. The next item she prepared was the green beans. She washed them and put them into a pot. Then, following the example her mother had set many times, she added her seasoning to the beans along with a ham hock for flavor. Finally, she had prepared the last item and it was ready to go onto the stove. She placed it on the stove and fired it up. Looking in on the cornbread, she saw that it was ready. She removed it from the oven, admiring its golden crust. The exterior of the ham was looking good also. She made a shallow cut to see how it looked on the inside. She figured it would probably only need about 15 more minutes. Once the fifteen minutes had elapsed, she took the ham out, put the birthday cake in, and turned down the temperature to the correct setting. The garden salad was the last item she prepared.

She finished it in just a few minutes. By this time, the potatoes had cooked. She removed them from the stove and began mashing them up. Next, she added seasoning and set them aside. The green beans were smelling really good. She checked them and they seemed to be done so she turned the heat off. It was about 5:30 p.m. and dinner usually started at 6 p.m. Rebecca thought she had pulled everything together just in time. The birthday cake was the only item left. About fifteen minutes later, it was also ready. She put it in the refrigerator to cool down a little before putting the icing and candles on. Rebecca was able to complete her first full course meal for her father's birthday at exactly 6:00 p.m. She proudly placed all of the food on the diningroom table except for the birthday cake. She placed it on the counter for everyone to see. Exhausted, she went to her room to change for dinner. When she finished, she went into the family room where everyone had gathered and announced that dinner was ready.

Rebecca had done a wonderful job setting the table. When her family entered the diningroom, they were very impressed. Before sitting down, they held hands and John said a prayer and blessed the meal. Rebecca was both excited and nervous. Everything looked and smelled really good, but she was more concerned with how it would taste. Her brother, John Jr., volunteered to slice the ham. The deeper he sliced, the rarer the ham became. Everyone started looking around at each other as John Jr. sliced layer upon layer of rare ham. At John's urging, John Jr. continued to slice the ham while Sarah began to pass the green beans. Next to travel around the table were the mashed potatoes. When the cornbread was passed, it seemed a little on the heavy side, but no one said a word.

Rebecca was busy serving up the garden salad and didn't immediately see their expressions. When she finished, she sat down at the table and realized what everyone else already knew. The ham was only cooked on the outside, the inside was raw. Her heart sank to the bottom of her stomach. She wanted to leave the room, but she couldn't. She wasn't beaming with excitement anymore. She felt as if a lead weight was pushing her down in her seat. She wanted to cry, but fought back her tears. John could see the hurt and disappointment on her face.

"Thanks for cooking my birthday meal. I'll never forget it," her father said, smiling.

"I'm sure you won't," Thomas cracked.

"That will be enough, Thomas," John said sternly. John began eating his birthday meal. Sarah and the rest of the family joined in. John started a conversation in an effort to ease the frustration that Rebecca was feeling.

The home style green beans, old fashioned mashed potatoes and garden salad were delicious. The cornbread was more than a little on the heavy side. It was downright dangerous. In her rush to make up time for starting late, she forgot to include the shortening. John knew something was wrong with it, but he was determined to eat it. He took his time and chewed it really well before swallowing. He ate at least one portion of everything Rebecca had prepared. The rest of the family finished long before John did. They were waiting for him to finish so they could see if the cake tasted as good as it looked. After he had his last bite, he placed his fork against the rim of his plate.

"It's dessert time," Robert said, hoping that the cake tasted better than the meal. Everyone helped clear the dishes while Rebecca placed the birthday cake on the table in front of John. Everyone was so excited. She lit the candles and stood back.

"Make a wish, daddy," his children told him. John closed his eyes, made a wish, and blew out the candles. He cut the cake and started serving up portions to his family while Rebecca went to the refrigerator and got the ice cream.

"Happy Birthday!" they exclaimed before they started eating the cake. When they bit into it, they realized something had been left out. Each of the family members placed their pieces back on the plate. John was the only one who continued to eat. He kept eating until his piece was gone.

When Rebecca came back with the ice cream, the room was deathly quiet."What's wrong?" Rebecca asked. She took a bite of the cake and realized she had left out the sugar. She couldn't believe she'd done that. It was too much! She couldn't hold back the tears any longer.

"I didn't do anything right," Rebecca yelled as she ran from the room. Concerned, Sarah went out behind her. A few minutes later, they returned to the diningroom. John Jr. walked over to his dad and wished him happy birthday. He handed John his gift. The rest of his siblings, except for Rebecca, followed suit. After John had opened all of their gifts, Rebecca told her father that she didn't have a gift for him.

"I forgot to get it," she explained. "I'll go and get one tomorrow," she promised as tears streamed down her face.

"Rebecca, honey, you don't have to do that," he said. "This day has been a special day for me and you have been a big part of it. The mere fact that you wanted to cook my birthday meal is a gift that I will always treasure. Any time a parent can share such a festive occasion with the ones he loves is very special indeed. As far as the meal is concerned, the beans, the salad, and the mashed potatoes were delicious. You're going to be a great cook someday, just like your mother," he told her as he winked at Sarah.

"If she doesn't kill someone first," Thomas joked.

"Be quiet, Thomas. No one asked for your opinion," Rebecca said, buoyed by her father's support.

"We can rescue the ham, but the cake and cornbread gotta go," Sarah told Rebecca, laughing.

When they retired for the night, John asked Sarah to bring something for his stomach.

"I think I'm going to need it," he said, thinking of all the ill-cooked food he had eaten that evening.

"That's my dad," Rebecca would later remember.

THOMAS RETURNED HOME

After they finished dinner, Sarah cleared the table and put the dishes in the dishwasher. John went into the family room and sat down in his favorite chair. When Sarah finished in the kitchen, she joined him. John was smiling as he looked through the family picture album. She sat down next to him. John turned the page and focused his thoughts onto Thomas, his second son, who had lost a leg in the Vietnam War.

"Do you remember how difficult it was when Thomas returned home from the war?"

"I'll never forget those days and nights," she said, remembering how spiritually wounded Thomas had been. He had come home from the war a defeated man. When he arrived at the airport, his parents were there to meet him.

Thomas' attitude had improved very little since their visit with him in the hospital a month before. He did manage a smile and hug for his parents, but after the greeting, no one knew what to say. The silence was deafening. Slicing through the ever-expanding quiet, John asked him how he was doing.

"I'm struggling really bad, dad. Some days are better than others, but most nights are terrifying. For the first time in my life, I don't know what to do," he explained tearfully. "At times, I can still feel my leg. If I said I'm okay, I'd be lying to you," he told his parents. His tears surprised him. He thought he'd gotten a hold on his emotions during the flight.

When they got home, John was parking the car in the driveway when Thomas' brothers and sisters came out to greet him. Right away they noticed something was different about Thomas. It wasn't the loss of his leg, but something else. They realized that his attitude had changed a lot. He seemed like a totally different person. They didn't know what to say or to do around him.

His trademark smile wasn't there anymore and he didn't talk very much. They were careful not to ask anything about his wound. He still sat with his family at dinner, but it wasn't the same as before. Although Sarah cooked his favorite foods, he ate very little and didn't comment on the food at all. He seemed to be in his own little world and he stood guard, not letting anyone in. When asked a question, he would answer it but no further conversation was forthcoming.

Before going to war, Thomas had been a gifted athlete. He had lettered in basketball, football, and baseball. He had wanted to go out for track and field, but his schedule wouldn't allow it. His room had been filled with all kinds of trophies, medals, and awards he had received during his high school and college days. When he went to the war, Sarah had left everything just as it was.

The first night Thomas was home had shocked and scared John and Sarah. They had never expected what happened. Around 1 a.m., the whole family was awakened by loud pounding and crashing sounds coming from Thomas' room. Alarmed, John and Sarah went to see what was happening. They found Thomas sitting on the floor. He had taken one of his crutches and destroyed all of his trophies, medals, and awards. Broken pieces lay scattered about him as he sat in the middle of it, crying like a child. He was a broken man.

Not knowing what else to do, John and Sarah pushed aside the broken pieces and sat down next to Thomas. "God has not abandoned you," they said as they held him, "We'll get through this."

Thomas' brothers and sisters had heard the commotion and were deeply affected by their brother's sadness. Knowing now was not the right time for a public display of support, they returned to their rooms and cried silent tears.

During the early morning hours, after everyone had gone back to sleep, Thomas walked out of the front door and locked it behind him. The flood of emotions had been too much for him to handle. Home was where he should have found peace and contentment. Instead, he was feeling the opposite. Everything around him was a reminder of the life he had planned so carefully. He had not found peace and contentment, but instead he was still suffering from depression and despair. The events of the war were still reaping havoc on his mind, especially the day he lost his best friend. The image of Allen's fallen body with his blood oozing out was tough for Thomas to deal with. The events of the war vividly played themselves out during the night and stayed on his mind during the day. He awoke most nights, calling his friend's name. He'd tell him that he was coming, but he could never get there. Just before he reached Allen, he would hear the explosion that had taken his leg and he would wake up.

He didn't want to go to sleep in his home. He was afraid he would scare his family again. He sat on the porch for several minutes. It was a beautiful starlit night. He had looked up to the heavens many times before and was amazed at how wonderful it looked. Before, he had felt so connected to life around him. Now, he felt disconnected and life seemed to be passing him by.

"God," he said, "if you can create something as intricate as the heavens, why didn't you help me?" He stood up on his broken crutches and started walking. He stopped in the middle of the road. Having looked one way and then the other, neither direction interested him, but there was a place that had never failed to bring him joy and peace. He began slowly moving in its direction. When he crossed the road, he looked back and saw Mack, the family dog, following him. He tried to make him turn back, but Mack was being less than cooperative.

Moving through the trees almost freaked him out. It reminded him of the ambushes he and his squad had gone on during his tour of duty. They had moved into their positions under the cover of darkness and waited for the enemy to come by so they could try to kill them. The place he was going was about a mile away. He was in no hurry to get there and stopped to rest a couple of times. He made it just before daylight. He sat down against his favorite tree, breathing in the crisp, fall air. It wasn't cold yet, but the air had a distinct chill to it. Thankfully, Thomas was wearing a coat. He reached into one of the pockets and took out a candy bar and began eating. Mack came over and sat down beside him. Thomas reached over and rubbed his head. They sat there together in total silence.

Thomas knew he had to get his emotions under control. He couldn't sleep and he wasn't thinking clearly. He felt helpless and hopeless. It would have been better if he had died on the battlefield. 'If I had,' he thought, 'all of my problems would be over.'

In the distance, he saw the bright rays of the sun moving up and over the horizon. It was such a radiant scene. Momentarily, it took him away from all of his problems. He watched as the sky took on an ethereal glow. Red and orange lit the sky.

Thomas was ashamed for people to see him especially his family and friends. He knew they were trying very hard to understand what he was going through. He also knew they couldn't understand unless they had experienced as violent a loss that he had.

Before the war, he had been so positive about the things he was going to achieve in life. Everything had gone according to plan until he entered the army. The plan called for two years of military service and then he would get on with his life. He never planned for this.

The day Thomas' unit was attacked, he went through a near death experience. They had a hot landing zone and they were unable to get Thomas to the field hospital for three hours. He almost bled to death. When he woke up in the hospital and was told his leg had to be amputated just below the knee, he felt as if the life had drained from his body. He looked down at his leg and told the doctor that he was mistaken.

"My leg is still here," he informed the doctor. "I can feel it," he insisted.

"It's not uncommon to feel a missing limb for a short period of time," the doctor responded.

Thomas was silent for a moment. "How is Allen?" he asked the doctor.

"He didn't make it, he died on the battlefield," the doctor told him softly. Thomas' heart dropped. He was totally unprepared for this.

"Maybe he's the lucky one. He doesn't have to worry about this madness anymore," he commented.

Thomas believed he had done everything right in his life and couldn't understand why things were falling apart. Something or someone had failed him. In both scenarios, God was the culprit. He was enraged with God and with life in general. His doctors were concerned about his negative attitude. Most of the care givers didn't want anything to do with him. He had a mean spirit and he was abusive.

When his parents arrived at the hospital to see him, they noticed the change in his demeanor. They were with him for several hours and he didn't smile once. He was depressed and seemed so distant. They tried everything to cheer him up, but nothing worked. They could not imagine what he had gone through since they saw him last. Thomas was uncooperative, even with his mother. When asked "stupid" questions, as he put it, by the doctors, he answered, "That doesn't deserve an answer."

One Tuesday morning, about a week into Thomas' recovery, a nurse named Stella started work on his floor. She always wore a smile and talked with the soldiers as she did her work. When she approached Thomas to take away his breakfast tray, he pushed it onto the floor. She picked it up, showing no signs that she heard it clatter to the floor, cleaned the floor, and continued on with her work. The next day, he did it again. They looked at each other, eye to eye, without exchanging a word. The other soldiers told her not to let him get under her skin.

Nurse Stella never complained. She kept smiling through it all. She didn't say anything to Thomas or treat him unkind in any way. On the third day, as she approached him, he started to knock over his tray, but stopped.

Aggravated at the smile on her face, he asked "What are you smiling about?"

"The Lord is good to me," she replied.

"I used to think that."

"What made you stop?" she asked as she took his tray.

"He abandoned me," Thomas told her.

"Are you sure about that?" she inquired, lifting her eyebrow at his statement.

"Yes, I'm sure. Take a look at me. Why do you think I'm here?"

"I think you're here because you need medical attention," she said, stating the obvious.

"He is the reason I need it," Thomas accused.

"God doesn't go around taking people's legs," she explained to him.

"That's easy for you to say. You have both of yours."

"Yes, I have both of mine. If I only had one, I wouldn't complain."

"How can you be so sure?" he asked, taking in her calm demeanor.

"Because I'm a Christian and I believe that God always wants the best for us," she said.

"He sure has a strange way of expressing it. Take a look around you," Thomas gestured toward the soldiers in the room.

"You're a Christian, right?" she asked Thomas.

"I used to be."

"Did you attend church on a regular basis?"

"Yes, I attended church and Sunday school. What's with all of the questions?" he ground out irritably. He didn't want to concede her point.

"Well, you should know that this is not the work of God, but of the fallen angel, Lucifer. If you aren't careful, he'll take more than just your leg, he'll take the rest of you," she warned. "I've got to go now," she said as she moved on.

Thomas didn't see Stella again for two whole days. By Monday morning, he was still bitter, but she had given him something to think about.

"Whose soul did you save this weekend, Christian?" he teased when he saw her approach.

"Only Jesus can save souls but, of course, you already know that. Don't you?" she replied with a smile. It was good to see some life in him.

"I don't know any such thing. He didn't save my leg or my friend, Allen," Thomas said with anger in his voice. It was too soon to forgive so much.

"You know better than most of the soldiers in here. Your bitterness has you in denial. Don't let the loss of your leg ruin the rest of your life," she admonished.

"Who are you to be preaching at me? What have you lost lately?" he asked bitterly. She was quiet for a moment and then she answered.

"I lost one of my brothers," she said quietly. Thomas could see her fighting back her tears as she continued. "I also lost my husband of ten years," she said. Her voice trailed off as she rushed off the floor.

Thomas had really stuck his foot in his mouth. The next day, a new nurse was assigned in Stella's place. He inquired about her and was told that she had been re-assigned to the seventh floor. Using his wheelchair, he took the elevator to the seventh floor nurse's station to see if she was there. One of the nurses directed him to her. She was working with a soldier who was lying in bed near a window. When he reached her, he said, "Hello, Christian."

She turned around, surprised, and asked him what he was doing on the seventh floor.

"I came to find you," he answered.

"What do you want with me, may I ask?"

"I want to apologize for my behavior on Monday."

"You don't have to. I understand" she told him genuinely.

"If you do, you should be my doctor instead of those quacks."

"You know, I don't even know your name," she admitted.

"Thomas Goodwin, at your service," he said with a smile. Making amends was hard work. He needed a little humor to make it easier.

"Mr. Goodwin, take a good look around you. These soldiers aren't capable of doing anything for themselves. Not only do they have physical wounds, but they and are also mentally disturbed. Many babble incoherently," she told him in an effort to get him to see outside of himself.

"Why are you working on this floor? Is it because of something I said on Monday?" he asked, dreading her response.

"No, I volunteered for this floor. This is where the demand for care is greatest. I feel like I'm making a difference here. These soldiers don't complain as much as the less injured," she said.

"You mean the ones like me, don't you?" he asked with more than a hint of remorse.

"You could say that," she answered.

Thomas took a deep breath. He felt awful for the way he had behaved. He was angry with God, not with Stella and he wanted her to understand that.

He'd had no reason to take his frustration out on her, except that she'd been available.

"Nurse Stella," Thomas said, "fighting in a war is nothing less than putting yourself through hell. In the process of destroying the bad people, you destroy a lot of innocent people along with them. Too often, the soldiers are maimed and crippled for life. The occupants of this floor can attest to that. I have seen enough to know the conditions of these men and women are much worst than mine. Try to understand my point of view. For the first time in my life, I don't know what to do. I made so many plans, just like most soldiers do before joining the military. Those of us who have suffered the loss of limbs, well, it's a condition that we can't fix. To fix it means to grow another limb and that's impossible. Our handicaps don't fit into our plans," Thomas explained emotionally.

"Mr. Goodwin, you must adjust your plans," Stella said. She would not allow him to feel sorry for himself. He had been doing that long enough.

"I don't know how. For the first time in my life, I'm afraid of being labeled a failure," he admitted.

"How did you receive your wounds?"

"I was trying to help my friend, Allen," he explained. He didn't want to remember that day. It was too much for him.

"Were you afraid?" she asked.

"No, I didn't have time to be afraid. I responded to his call for help."

"You have to muster the same kind of courage and strength for yourself. Now you must save yourself," she advised.

Thomas became aware of the tears rolling down his cheeks. He had not realized that he was crying. "I've tried, but I can't seem to find a way," he told her in despair. This conversation was draining what little energy he had left. "I'll see you later," he told her as he rolled toward the elevator.

"Please wait, Mr. Goodwin," Stella said. She could see the toll this was taking on him. His face was ashen beneath the tears rolling steadily down his cheeks. "I know everyone in the hospital is broken in different ways. There is no such thing as a little hurt when you're dealing with people's lives. I'm sorry if I gave you that impression. What I'm trying to emphasize to you is that you should not give up on life. Don't let this war do any more damage to you. You and these soldiers have sacrificed enough," she explained.

"Why do you continue to come to this place to work? There must be another job you could get that's not as gruesome as this one," he asked.

"I really care about the soldiers. Maybe this is my way of fighting back. You see, I have been wounded too," she reminded him.

"Yes, I'm sorry about your brother and your husband," he told her.

"I know you are. I'm sorry about the loss of your leg and your friend," she responded.

"Thanks," he said and left the floor. It was the first time since before the war that he'd met anyone on common ground, acknowledging an experience other than his own.

The doctors determined that they had done all they could for Thomas at the present time. They decided to let him go home to visit his family before proceeding further with his rehabilitation. They were hoping he would be more cooperative after his visit.

Thomas decided to go and say goodbye to Stella. When he arrived on her floor, he greeted her politely, if not somewhat shyly. He had shared a good bit of his soul with her. That was no easy accomplishment. He told her of the doctors' decision to let him go home for a while.

"Are you excited about that?" she asked.

"No, not really. I'm not ready to face them. Hell, I haven't even faced myself yet."

"Why do you feel that way?"

"I don't know how they will respond to me," he told her. For some reason, he found it easy to confide in her. He'd started to consider her a friend.

"You mean because of your leg?"

"Yes, I don't want to be treated like a helpless cripple. I know I look like a cripple, but I don't want to be treated like one," he told her emphatically.

"Mr. Goodwin, they will see you as you are. If you act like a cripple, they will treat you as one. They will react to the image and demeanor that you project. In other words, you will determine the way people treat you," she assured him.

"I know my family will be supportive and overbearing with compassion. Compassion is one of those things that makes me very uncomfortable. You see, I set such lofty goals for myself. All of my plans included all of me, not bits and pieces. I lived such a physical life. Now, I don't know what I'm capable of doing. I'm ashamed to face my family and friends."

"Mr. Goodwin, don't try to solve all of your problems at once," Stella said as she walked him to the elevator. You have to take life one day at a time. I'm sure if you do that, you'll be just fine."

"I wish I was as sure about it as you seem to be."

"You'll find the strength, just give yourself time."

"I'm going to try," he committed. They said goodbye to each other and Thomas returned to his floor. He started packing the few items he had for his departure home. Emotionally, he looked at all of the broken bodies that were around him. He had long ago began referring to it as the human junk yard. He had been careful not to make any friends while he was here. He was anxious about leaving and was uncertain about what lay ahead. When he called his parents, he asked them not to tell anyone but his family that he was coming home. He just couldn't deal with a lot of people right now. He had too much to sort out.

From the time he left the hospital, people started asking questions and staring at him. This made Thomas very uncomfortable. He was not used to this kind of attention. On the plane ride home, a little boy was seated across the aisle from him. The boy kept asking him what happened to his leg. He was really starting to annoy the hell out of Thomas. His mother tried to stop him, but he continued asking the question. Thomas tried to ignore him, but he was relentless with his questioning. Other passengers began looking in his direction so he finally decided to tell him, hoping that he would shut up. When he explained what happened, he was overheard by some of the passengers. Instead of putting it to rest, his explanation started a new question and answer session.

Most of the passengers were supportive of the war. All were supportive of the soldiers and their sacrifices. Thomas hadn't intended to engage in a full-blown conversation about the war. He turned away and stared out of the window of the plane, waiting for them to take the hint. The flight home was proving to be very difficult for Thomas. 'Home is where the heart is and maybe this will be the turning point on my road to recovery,' he thought. Later, he would discover that turning the switch on to war is much easier than turning it off. The healing that he needed would be elusive and would take a bit of soul searching.

THOMAS DISAPPEARS

The morning after Thomas' bitter rage in the middle of the night, Sarah made breakfast and called out to John and their children that breakfast was ready. Everyone but Thomas came.

"He's probably still asleep. I'll go and check on him," Sarah said as she went to Thomas' room. When Sarah entered his room, he wasn't there. She called to him, but there was no answer. They searched around the farm, but he was no where to be found. John went to some of their neighbors to see if anyone had seen Thomas. He had no luck as most said that they hadn't known that Thomas was home.

No one had seen him. One of the neighbors went with John to look for Thomas. They searched the nearby roads, but they didn't find him. It seemed as if Thomas had disappeared into thin air.

When John returned home, he and Sarah went to Thomas' room. They stared at the broken pieces lying on the floor and wondered where Thomas could be.

"Oh, Lord, protect him and let him come home safely," Sarah prayed. John and Sarah didn't sleep very much that night. They tried to figure out why Thomas had left in the middle of the night without telling them where he was going.

Around five o'clock the next morning, John went to Thomas' room, hoping that he had returned. He had not. Sarah awoke around six and began making breakfast. She made a cup of coffee for herself and one for John. It would be a long day.

"I hope Thomas hasn't done anything to hurt himself," she worried to John.

"I don't think he would do anything like that," John assured her as he patted her hand. John took his cup of coffee out on the front porch and sat down. He saw Mack, the family dog, next to a line of trees in the field across the road.

Mack was coming toward the house. He came up on the porch and lay down near John's feet. John didn't think much about it until about an hour later when Mack got up, after having had his breakfast of course, and started back across the road in the direction of the trees. Curious, John decided to follow him and see where he was going. Mack went straight to Thomas, he was sitting near one of the fishing ponds he used to frequent when he was a young boy. When John saw Thomas, he let out a sigh of relief. Thomas and Mack were sitting against the very tree that Thomas had claimed as his very own. He remembered Thomas saying, "this is my tree, daddy," when they came to this spot to fish, just the two of them.

John was trying to decide what to do. Thomas hadn't heard him approach and didn't know that he was there. John was careful not to attract his attention. Mack turned and looked in John's direction, as if to let him know that he knew he was there, but Mack didn't bark. He didn't make a sound.

John realized that Thomas had to sort things out on his own. He knew that, sometimes, a person really needs time alone with a good friend like Mack. He decided to leave Thomas alone. He could see that Thomas was okay. He would be fine unless it started to rain. John returned home and told Sarah and the family where Thomas was. Immediately, they all wanted to go and bring him home, but John told them it was not a good idea.

"Why not?" they asked him.

"Thomas didn't leave to get away from us," he explained. "He left because he's frustrated and confused. He needs time to sort things out for himself. We must allow him that time. I know you want to help him, but he must first learn to help himself. He'll come home when he's ready."

"What if something happens to him or he gets too weak to make it back on his own? How will we know?" they pressed him.

"I have a feeling he'll make it back, "John assured them.

As evening approached, John was hoping Thomas would return, but he didn't. John and his family had another restless night. When morning came, John took his coffee to the front porch and sat down. Sarah joined him a couple of minutes later.

"Do you think he's still at the pond?" she asked.

"I think he's still there."

"I sure hope he's all right," Sarah replied.

Sarah was really nervous. She couldn't sit still for long. She got to her feet and went back inside. John started to wonder if he'd made the right decision.

In the distance, he saw Mack coming toward the house alone. Like the day before, he came up on the porch and laid down at John's feet. John went in the house and brought out food and water for him. Mack stayed a couple of hours and then got up and headed back to Thomas.

"You take care of Thomas, you hear?" John called out to Mack. Mack stopped, turned around, barked and continued on his way.

John tried to go about his normal routine, but he was very uncomfortable. Sarah kept asking him what he would do if something happened to Thomas.

"I know he's hungry. He's probably too weak to walk back home," she worried. John assured her that if Thomas wasn't back by morning, he would go and get him.

"Do you think we should wait that long?" she asked.

"We have to give him enough time to make it back. It's very important to Thomas," John stressed to her.

"I sure hope you're right, John," she sighed.

When the night came and there was no sign of Thomas, the family started to believe John had made the wrong decision. They wouldn't tell him, but they had started to believe it. When they retired for the night, John acquiesced and told Sarah he would go and get Thomas in the morning.

On the fourth day of Thomas' disappearance, John and Sarah went to his room to see if he had returned during the night. He was not there. Sarah couldn't hold back her emotions any longer. She started crying and pleaded with John to go and get Thomas right away. John told Sarah he was going to get him. He walked out on the front porch and looked toward the pond to see if he could see Mack or Thomas coming. He waited about an hour, but Mack was not in sight. He paced the floor, wondering if he had waited too long. He finished his cup of coffee and went in to get another.

"What are you waiting for?" Sarah asked him. She'd thought that he would have already left.

"I'm waiting to see if Mack and Thomas are coming across the field," he told her. He felt it was very important to give Thomas the time he needed. Another half an hour passed. John decided he had waited long enough. As he got up to go inside for the keys to his truck, he again looked across the field in the direction of the fishing pond. He thought he saw a glimpse of Mack emerging from the tree line. He decided to wait for Mack to get to the house so he could take the dog with him.

When Mack was a few feet from the tree line, a big smile crossed John's face. Thomas was not far behind Mack. He watched as Thomas emerged from the tree line, hopping along on his broken crutches. He wasn't moving very fast, but John knew he was finally coming home.

"Thank you, Lord and I praise your name!" John exclaimed as he went inside and told Sarah and the family that Thomas was coming home.

"Let's go and help him!" they said excitedly.

"No, we can't. Let him get here on his own," John advised. They all stayed inside and watched Thomas through the windows.

"Come on, Thomas," they said among themselves, "you can make it."

Thomas stopped to rest a couple of times, but he finally made it to the front yard.

"Let's go out and welcome Thomas home," John said. They walked out to meet Thomas. John could tell from the expression on his face that some of the bitterness was gone. Thomas had a smile on his face. Everyone told him they had been extremely worried about him.

"I didn't mean to worry you," Thomas apologized. "I had to get away. Coming home just brought back so many memories, so many emotions. I know I have problems. I'm really trying to learn to deal with them."

"That's exactly what you gotta do, son," John said as he patted Thomas' shoulder. "If you continue to be bitter, you will eventually destroy yourself. This is not the end, but a new beginning. Don't concentrate on what was taken away, concentrate on what you have left. Ask God to help you understand your possibilities and the direction your life must take from here," John explained to Thomas.

After Thomas had gone in the house, John looked around for Mack and their eyes met. Mack went up on the porch, had his breakfast, and fell asleep.

Being at the fishing pond had really helped Thomas. He had lost some of the bitterness and resentment he'd been harboring inside. He still had a long way to go to accept his physical condition and start to rebuild his life.

He slowly let his family become a part of his life again. He realized he had been trying to punish them along with everyone else he came in contact with. He eventually opened up to his family. There were many tears shed. He told them about the events leading up to the crucial battle. When he started talking, it seemed like the wall he had built to hide behind finally came crumbling down. His family watched and listened in amazement as Thomas poured out his heart to them.

"Allen was my best friend. We shared some of the same hopes and dreams," he said.

"What happened to him?" Robert asked.

"He died the day we made our last combat assault. I stepped on a land mine trying to save him," he told his family.

The next day, John asked his family if they would like to prepare a picnic lunch for the whole family to go on an outing at the fishing pond. They were all in favor of his suggestion. Two days later, John took his family to the fishing pond that Thomas liked so well. Of course, Mack went along with them. He ran along side the truck.

They were able to catch several fish. Every time one of them were pulled out of the water, Mack got really excited and started barking and carrying on like he was the one who'd caught it. It was a beautiful day and it was one of the most enjoyable days the Goodwin family had ever experienced. Thomas rediscovered the love and support his family shared with each other and the abiding faith they had in the goodness of God.

On Sunday morning, the Goodwins went to church. Thomas was a little apprehensive about seeing his friends and neighbors, but his parents assured him that everything would be all right. His siblings reminded him that the Goodwins always stuck together and this time was no different.

"You don't have to worry about a thing. We'll be there with you," Rebecca said.

John had bought Thomas a new pair of crutches on Saturday and Thomas used them to go to church on Sunday. They went in two cars because it was too many of them to go in one. Thomas rode with John Jr., Robert, and Mary. They talked on the way there, but they could tell Thomas was a little uncomfortable.

There were a lot of people standing around outside when they drove into the parking lot. John Jr. and Mary got out of the car and waited for Thomas. Thomas didn't want to get out, but they encouraged him to. The rest of the family walked over to where they were parked and waited for them so they could all go in together. When the people recognized who he was, they started gathering around him. The minister walked over, shook his hand, and told him how glad he was to see him. His family was right by his side.

Just as they entered the church sanctuary, someone reached over and caught his arm. It was his friend, Jason. Thomas hadn't seen Jason since college. He told Thomas that he was sorry about his leg.

"How long have you been here?" Thomas asked him, changing the subject.

"Two days now. My parents' health isn't too good," Jason explained. "How long for you?"

"I've been home about a week."

"You okay?" Jason asked him. He wasn't fooled by Thomas' attempt to avoid what had happened to him. He remembered the young man Thomas had been in college. He had to be taking this hard.

"Jason, it's been extremely difficult for me. The war was pure hell. I have never been through anything as hard as that war," Thomas told Jason.

"Can we talk after the service?" Jason asked.

"Sure we can," Thomas replied. It would be good to have a friend again.

The Goodwins took their seats just before the service started. Thomas sat on the end of the pew next to the aisle. When the time came for the guests to be recognized, the pastor told the congregation that one of their own had returned from the war as a hero.

"I want you to give brother Thomas Goodwin a hero's welcome," he told them. The congregation stood and applauded loud and long. They were trying to show their appreciation for the sacrifice he had made for his country.

Thomas didn't feel like a hero. He knew they all meant well, but he couldn't let that stand. There was something that rose up on the inside of him and lifted him to his feet.

When the applause stopped, Thomas was already on his crutches. He addressed the congregation on behalf of the real heros. "I appreciate the warm welcome you have given me today," he said. "There were times when I thought I would never have the opportunity to worship with you again. I don't consider myself a hero though. Heros are people who are willing to put their lives on the line, knowing that there is a possibility of losing it. I want to tell you about a real hero and there are many just like him. His name was Allen Jefferson. He was a young man about my age. He had hopes and dreams just like all of us," Thomas pressed on tearfully. "He attended church with his family on a regular basis. He had a loving and caring family that prayed for his safe return. He had no brothers and one sister and he often spoke of the influence his grandparents had on his life. His grandparents have handicaps, they were involved in a serious car accident, but he admired their courage. They were able to adjust to the way their lives were changed and maintain their independence. Allen had a bright future and would have achieved great things in his life. You see," he said, choking back his tears, "Allen and thousands of young men and women won't be able to attend church anymore. I'm wounded, but I came back home alive. Eventually, I'll find my way again. They're coming home in body bags. Oh yes, they will enter their church, but it will be for the last time. Their congregations and their loved ones will be saying goodbye. Those are the ones that deserve to be called heros. I'm not worthy of the title. Please, remember them and their loved ones in your prayers." After Thomas finished pouring his heart out, he sat down. He was exhausted.

Understanding Thomas' sentiment, the minister once again led the congregation in applause. "All of you young men and women seated in this sanctuary and the rest of us, just heard some words of wisdom from brother Goodwin. When you care about the welfare of others, it helps you develop character and integrity. We heard from a man who has gone through a great deal of difficulty. He has shown compassion for his wounded and fallen comrades," he continued as he made direct eye contact with Thomas. "In this sanctuary, the gospel is preached every Sunday. Today, we saw the gospel on the face of brother Goodwin and we heard its reality in his words. A greater love has no man than that he lay down his life for another. Brother Goodwin, I pray for God to bless you with his very best. I'll be praying that he makes his face to shine upon you in all of your endeavors."

By the end of the service, anyone who hadn't known Thomas knew who he was. Most of the community hadn't known he was home until that day. They praised him for the statement he made on behalf of his fellow soldiers.

While he was speaking with his neighbors, someone patted him on his back. When he turned around, he saw an old lady with a smile on her face. It was Mrs. Katherine Turner. Thomas had maintained her yard from the time he was ten years old until he went away to college.

"Hi, Thomas. Do you remember me?" she asked him.

"Mrs. Turner, I sure do," he said, bending so she could hug him. "I'll never forget you. I'll always remember those lunches we had when I was doing your yard," he said.

"My yard has never looked as good since you stopped doing it," she said.

Thomas took in her appearance. She was a proud, regal woman. Her hair had turned gray long ago. He could see it gracefully arranged beneath her white church hat.

"How are you doing, Mrs. Turner? It is so good to see you," he said.

"I'm getting along pretty well for an old woman. I get up every day and do the best that I can and leave the rest up to the Lord. How are you coping with the change in your life?" she asked.

"I can't lie to you, Mrs. Turner, I've had a really difficult time dealing with what has happened to me and my friend." He allowed her to take his arm as they headed out of the church.

"Thomas, my boy, have faith in God that he will see you through this most difficult time in your life and bring you out on the other side. Don't blame him for your troubles. He is not responsible for them. All hands and legs are his and everything else. He can take them all if he wants to. He doesn't operate that way. He always wants the best for his children and you are one of his children," she said.

"Mrs. Turner, you have always given me sound advice. Deep down in my soul, I know what you're saying is true. I'll recover, but I'm struggling right now."

"That's understandable," she said as she patted his arm. "You have experienced a lot of trauma since leaving here. Come down, I have something for you," she said. Thomas bent over, thinking she had something to tell him in private. As he leaned down, she kissed him on the cheek. "God loves you and so do I," she said as she patted his cheek. "Come to see me if you have time before you leave. I want you to cut my grass," she told him. They both laughed. "I'm going home, now," she said and made her way toward her car.

Thomas watched the ninety-year-old woman move with grace and dignity with the aid of her walking cane as she walked to her car. She got in the passenger seat of a car parked nearby and one of her nephews drove her home.

As he walked outside, he saw Jason in the parking lot, waiting. They had a few minutes to talk before they left for their respective homes.

"How did you like church today, Thomas?" John asked him.

"It was quite an experience, dad. It was good seeing family and friends again. Mrs. Turner doesn't seem to age at all," Thomas reflected.

"She does seem to be in remarkable health. I'm sure she has overcome many difficulties in her lifetime. As we age, I think we develop more patience and we learn to wait on the Lord. I believe that is one of the reasons for her long life," John explained.

"Thomas, how long do you have before you have to report back?" Sarah inquired.

"I have three more weeks. I'm going to North Carolina to see Allen's family. It's something I feel I must do. I want to explain to them what happened the day he was killed. Maybe I will be able to help them understand things better," Thomas told his dad.

"When are you going to leave?" John asked. He was proud of his son for taking this step.

"I think I'll leave tomorrow. I'll be gone for three or four days," Thomas said.

Later, he called Allen's parents and explained to them who he was. He found out that Allen had mentioned Thomas in his letters to his family. Thomas asked them if he could come and visit them for a few days. They assured him that he would be welcome to stay as long as he wanted to. He told them he would let them know about the flight plans as soon as he made them.

When the time came, Thomas asked his dad for a ride to the airport. "Will you take me to the airport tomorrow, dad?" he asked after he finished his conversation.

"I'll be glad to take you, son."

Thomas had called and made reservations on an evening flight to Charlotte, North Carolina. He called Allen's parents and gave them the name of the airline, the flight number, and the time of arrival. They asked him to describe himself so they would be able to recognize him.

"I'll be easy to recognize," he said. "I'll be the one on the crutches with half his right leg missing," he said, instantly realizing how harsh he sounded.

Allen's father didn't miss a beat. "We're sorry to hear that. We didn't know you were wounded," he said.

"I know you didn't, sir," Thomas replied, feeling instantly contrite.

"We'll be waiting at the airport for you, Thomas," Mr. Jefferson said before hanging up the telephone.

Thomas and his parents left for the airport at 10 a.m. the next morning. It was a three-way conversation the whole way there. The trip seemed shorter this time. When they arrived at the airport, he got out of the car and told his parents he would be okay and that they could go home.

"I'll call you later to let you know when to pick me up," he promised.

"We'll see you later son," they said. He waved as they drove away.

Thomas had dressed in civilian clothes so that he wouldn't draw as much attention as he had before. When he boarded the plane for Charlotte, his mind was focused on the memories he had of Allen. They'd only known each other for a short period of time, but the impact their relationship would have on Thomas' life would last a lifetime. He was on his way to meet a family that would enlighten him in many ways.

When the plane landed, Thomas walked to the baggage area where he was supposed to meet

Mr. Jefferson. Thomas was standing at the carousel waiting for his bag to make the trip around when someone said, "you must be Thomas."

Turning around, he said, "Yes, I am. Are you Mr. Jefferson?"

"Yes," the man replied as he extended his hand to Thomas. They shook hands and greeted each other. Thomas looked back at the carousel in time to grab his bag before it got away from him. Before he reached it, Mr. Jefferson grabbed the bag and told Thomas that he would carry it.

"That won't be necessary," Thomas informed him.

"I insist, please come this way," Mr. Jefferson replied.

Mr. Jefferson led the way to the parking space where he had parked his car. He walked slowly so Thomas could keep up. When they finally reached the car, Thomas was exhausted. There was no way he would have made it if he had carried his own bag.

"Are you okay?" Mr. Jefferson asked.

"Yes, I am. I'm a little tired though. I can't seem to get used to these things," he said as he motioned to the crutches.

"Don't ever get used to them," Mr. Jefferson advised. "You won't need them very long. You'll be walking without them soon."

When they got settled in the car, Mr. Jefferson turned the ignition and began backing out of the parking space. "Allen was our only son. I didn't want him to serve in the military for fear that something like this would happen. He wanted to go to help support this great country of ours," Mr. Jefferson explained. "When did you meet him?" he asked.

"We met in basic training. We were in different platoons, but in the same company."

"What was he like in the military?"

"He was always enthusiastic about whatever he was doing. There was something different about Allen. I noticed it right away," Thomas told him.

"Allen was always so passionate about life. He was born after my wife had three miscarriages. He was a quick study on just about everything he tried," Mr. Jefferson reminisced.

"Well, he was the best friend I ever had. In war, you feel down at times, I don't care how positive on life you are. There are elements of danger that persist at all times. You have to learn to deal with it the best you can. Allen and I used to confide in each other. When things weren't going well, we tried to cheer each other up."

A little while later, they pulled up to the Jefferson home. "We're here," Mr. Jefferson told him. He pulled the car into the garage and they both got out.

"Thomas, Allen's death has devastated my family. All three of us have been struggling with it ever since we were notified. He filled this house with so much joy and now it feels empty without him. I wanted you to know this before meeting my wife and daughter," he explained.

Mr. Jefferson opened the door and called out, "we're here." Thomas came in behind him and closed the door. His wife, Clair, and their daughter, Maria, came from another room to greet them. When they saw Thomas standing with his crutches and part of his amputated leg, tears came to their eyes. He began to wonder if he had made a mistake coming here.

"I'm Thomas Goodwin," he told them. "I'm a friend of Allen's."

"We know who you are Mr. Goodwin," Clair Jefferson said with a smile on her face. "Please, have a seat. Allen told us in his letters that you would come to visit us if he didn't make it back. He thought very highly of you," she said as he sat down.

"Please, call me Thomas, Mrs. Jefferson, Allen and I had an agreement. We promised each other if one of us didn't make it back, the survivor would visit the family of the deceased. If we both made it back safely, we planned to visit each other's family after the war was over. I hope my being here doesn't make things worse," Thomas stated.

"Thomas, we want to know what Allen went through on the day of his death. Will you please tell us what happened?" Mrs. Jefferson asked with tears in her eyes.

"I'll tell you," Thomas said as he began to tear up. He'd been dreading this moment. He knew it would come sooner than later and, although he hated to think of that day, he had made a promise to Allen and he was going to honor his word.

"We were informed two days earlier that we were going south on a 90-day mission. We were told it was a hot area for the north Vietnamese army. The day before we made the combat assault, we spent all day on the planes in order to reach the staging area. Allen and I talked things over the night before. We talked about the things we were going to do when we returned to civilian life. We reminisced about how our lives had been before we entered the military. We made the agreement that I mentioned to you earlier. We were trying to find a little peace and contentment in the midst of all the death and destruction surrounding us.

We acknowledged the important roles our families had played in our lives, we talked about the richness of life, the kind that money can't buy and only God can provide. We both realized it can only be found in the families who put God first and become part of his Christian family. We wanted to be one of those who enter into this kingdom and make him the center of their lives. We knew we were each blessed with that type of family. We knew we had experienced that richness and we were fighting in a war in a far away land in the hope that the Vietnamese people would someday have the opportunity to experience it too. When we finished the conversation, we said a prayer for protection. We had been through a lot of tough battles, but we knew this last one had the potential of being really bad. We always looked out for each other the best we could.

The next morning, before dawn, everyone was awakened and told to prepare to move out at daylight. We could hear the B-52s bombing the valley as we prepared to be airlifted."

THE DAY ALLEN DIED

"Allen and I were in the lead company in the assault," Thomas continued. "When the helicopters arrived, Allen and his platoon were the first to board. On his way to the chopper, he gave me a thumbs up and I returned it. When the rest of the company reached the drop off point, Allen and his platoon were engaged in a fierce fire fight. The intelligence report had been accurate. They were dug in and waiting for us. Although the B-52s bombed the area early that morning, they failed to deliver the knock out blow they had hoped for. Allen and his platoon took the full impact of the assault because they were the first to land.

It was a very hot day. The temperature had to be around 100 degrees or better. We were not used to that type of heat. Before going south, we had operated in the mountains under the forest canopy. Several of the troops suffered from heat exhaustion. As we moved to our objective, we were constantly under attack. We continued fighting and pushing our enemy back. They were the toughest units we had fought against but we were up to the challenge.

From what you have told me about Allen, Mr. Jefferson, he was true to form that day. The way he maneuvered his troops, he saved many lives. Several soldiers were pinned down in an open field and were taking on casualties. Allen and I took four soldiers and flanked the enemy position to the right along a tree line.

We were undetected until we were right on them. They were so surprised to see us coming that most of them ran, but not all of them. The ones that stayed turned their weapons in our direction and continued firing. We were able to get most of them before we suffered any casualties. We took out two positions and gave chase to the ones that ran. The soldiers that were pinned down were able to cross the open field in safety. We continued pursuing the enemy until we encountered a fortified gun position. Two of our soldiers were hit and it was difficult to get to them.

We all carried smoke grenades as part of our equipment. So we decided to throw red smoke as close to the position as possible to cover our movement and take the position. After throwing the smoke, Allen gave a thumbs up and we threw live grenades and charged the position. Allen was leading the way," Thomas said and paused. His emotions were catching up with him. In a much lower and slower tone, he explained what happened next. "Just before Allen entered the red smoke, he was hit with gun fire and went down. He called out for someone to help him. I was rushing to aid him when I heard a loud blast. I was catapulted into the air and slammed against the ground. I lost consciousness and didn't come to until I was in the hospital."

"What happened to you Thomas?" Mr. Jefferson asked him.

"I stepped on a land mine. The doctors had to amputate my leg to save my life. When I woke up in the hospital, I was told that Allen had died on the battlefield. I couldn't believe that he was gone. It just didn't seem real."

"How are you doing with your injury?" Mrs. Jefferson asked as she wiped tears away.

"Ever since that dreadful day, I have struggled with the reality of what has happened."

"God is a good God, he'll see you through this," Maria told him.

"Please forgive me, Maria. Thomas, this is Maria, our daughter," Mrs. Jefferson said as she motioned to Maria, formally introducing them for the first time.

"I'm pleased to meet you, Maria," Thomas addressed her.

"Allen wrote of you often in his letters. I'm so glad you were able to share with us what happened. The military just informs you that your loved one has been fatally wounded. They don't give the details like you just did," Maria explained.

"Maybe this information will help make it easier to put closure on this tragedy, but not on Allen's life. His memory will last forever," Thomas told them. They were all in agreement.

"Allen loved talking about his grandparents. I would very much like to meet them," Thomas requested.

"We'll take you to meet them tomorrow. Come, let me show you to the room you'll sleep in while you're here," Mr. Jefferson said as he took Thomas' bag and led him down a hallway to his room. Before entering, he pointed to the room next to it and told Thomas that it had been Allen's room. He gave

Thomas permission to look inside, if he wished, then invited him down to have supper when he was ready.

"Do you need anything for your leg?" he inquired.

"No, I'm fine for now. I have to keep the bandages changed and be careful not to re-injure it. It's healing quite well," Thomas assured him.

At supper, Thomas explained to the Jefferson family that he'd been plagued by nightmares since the battle. He warned them that he might have one while he was there.

"Please forgive me if I do," Thomas requested of them.

"If you need assistance in any way while you're here, we'll help in any way we can," Mrs. Jefferson offered.

After supper, they sat around talking until it was time for bed. Thomas returned to his room, but he was not sleepy so he watched television for a while. He wanted to have a look inside of Allen's room, but he didn't want to disturb the family so he waited until he thought they were sound asleep.

When he opened the door to Allen's room, he was surprised to see Mrs. Jefferson sitting on the bed, looking at Allen's pictures as tears filled her eyes. Apologizing, he started to close the door. "Please, don't leave. Come on in, Thomas. Sometimes, when I can't sleep, I come in here," she explained.

"I wasn't sleepy either. I couldn't stand being so close to the room that Allen spent so much time in without coming in to see it for myself. I feel like he was one of my brothers. You know, he was like a member of my family. I wish we had met a long time ago or that the war had turned out differently for both of us. Looking around this room," he said, noticing a picture of an elderly couple smiling on a hot, summer day, "I can feel the love and the passion for life that he exuded. Is that a picture of his grandparents? He often spoke so affectionately of them."

"Yes, it is," she said as she handed him the photograph so he could take a better look. "That picture was taken before the accident. You know, both of them almost died in that crash. One of the reasons we all love and admire them so much is because of the courage they showed in caring for themselves after leaving the hospital. They were determined to maintain their independence. They have their struggles, but they manage just fine. You'll meet them tomorrow."

"Are they your parents?" Thomas asked.

"Yes, they are. Charlie's parents are both dead," she said as she pointed to another picture hanging on the wall. "That's them. They died when Allen was a young boy. He didn't remember much about them. He grew up around my parents and he adored his grandfather, Jacob, and his grandmother, Isabelle."

After an extended pause, she told him she was going to bed. She rose to leave the room. She sensed that he needed some time to himself. "You stay as long as you like," she said and then she was gone.

Thomas stayed there for a while. He noticed a Bible that lay opened on a night stand near the bed. He picked it up and saw that Psalm 23 had been underlined and the fourth verse had been circled. He read aloud:

> "Yea, though I walk through the valley of the shadow of death, I will fear no evil; for thou art with me: thy rod and thy staff they comfort me."

Thomas was encouraged by what he had found in Allen's room. He returned to his room and, for the first time since the night before the battle, he lowered himself down on his knees and acknowledged the sovereignty of God in a prayer. He asked God to forgive him for the anger and bitterness he'd displayed against him. He took his time and talked to God as a son talks to his father. There was so much to say. He hadn't prayed in a long time and he had carried the burdens of war too long. He asked God to please take it all away. When he finished, he rose slowly with tears in his eyes. He turned out the light and went to sleep.

The next morning, Maria made breakfast for everyone. Normally, Thomas was an early riser, but not this morning. He found himself startled awake by a knock on the door.

"What time is it?" he asked.

"It's nine o'clock. Are you all right?" Maria asked as she poked her head in the room.

"Yes, I'm okay. Thanks for asking. I'll be right out," he said. When he came out of his room, the family was sitting around watching television. They greeted him good morning and returned with him to the breakfast table. They asked Thomas to say grace. He agreed and they all bowed their heads.

Thomas didn't just bless the food and say Amen, he petitioned God to bless the food for the nourishment of their bodies. He believed this was an excellent opportunity to reach out to the Jefferson family. They were hurting and maybe this was the reason Allen had wanted him to come and visit with them. Before he went any further, he asked everyone to hold hands. He prayed a deep and lengthy prayer asking God to remove their hurt and pain, to give them the strength to let Allen go, knowing that he had made his journey home and that all was well with his soul. "We know he is there with you, Heavenly Father, and we also know that there is no greater place that he could be. Thank you, Amen."

Everyone raised their heads and smiled at Thomas. Mrs. Jefferson thanked him for such an eloquent prayer. Mr. Jefferson and Maria voiced their sentiments also. Thomas had done something important that morning. He took his eyes off of himself and his problems and reached out to help a hurting family. In doing so, he helped himself as well.

Reaching out to God the night before had made this possible. His parents had always told him that prayer changes things. He had turned back to the solid foundation that had always served his family well. His father had often told his children, "On that solid rock I stand, all else is shifting sand." Thomas realized there was no one else he could reach out to that would give the Jeffersons the hope they needed. He had to rely on the core principles his parents had taught him as a child. He knew he had been standing on shifting sand and that was why, spiritually, he had been sinking lower and lower. He realized it now because he could see the same thing happening to Allen's family. He was moved with compassion to try to help them.

After breakfast, Maria volunteered to take Thomas over to visit with her grandparents. Mr. and Mrs. Jefferson couldn't go with them, they had an appointment that they had to keep. On the way there, Maria told Thomas about the close relationship she'd had with her brother and how much she missed him. She took him by the church and told him how helpful and supportive their church family had been to them.

"I don't believe we would have made it if they hadn't been there for us," she said.

Next, she took him by the high school Allen attended and the YMCA where he often worked with young children. He had been a mentor for many of them. They had taken his death pretty hard. Thomas and Maria continued their conversation as she drove to her grandparents home.

"We're here," she said as she turned into the driveway. Right away, Thomas noticed the wheelchair ramp leading down to the ground on the right side of the porch. Other than that, everything else was normal. There was a van in the driveway that looked normal but on a closer inspection, he observed the modification of all the controls up near the steering wheel. It also had a lift on the driver's side. On second thought, there was nothing normal about the van.

Maria rang the doorbell and when the door was opened, there stood an older gentleman on crutches with braces on both of his legs. He had a wide smile on his face. He welcomed Maria and Thomas in and introduced himself as Grandpa Jacob.

"You must be Thomas Goodwin?" he asked.

"Yes, I am sir," Thomas responded.

"Please, call me Grandpa Jacob. Allen mentioned you in his letters, young man."

"He often spoke of his Grandpa Jacob as well," Thomas said with a smile.

"My grandson was something special. Before he went to the war, we talked every day. I hated to see him go, but I guess it was his destiny to be there. How are you doing, son? I see you and I have something in common," Grandpa Jacob said as he looked down at Thomas' leg.

"Yes, we do. We seem to be brothers of the same lodge," Thomas answered. Grandpa Jacob burst out in a booming laugh. It was infectious and Maria and Thomas found themselves laughing along with him.

"Son, you have the right attitude about life. You're going to be just fine. You can't take your setbacks too seriously. You have to laugh as often as you can. Life is too short to go around licking your wounds every day," Grandpa Jacob said as he lead them through the livingroom.

"Where is grandma?" Maria asked.

"She's out back tending to her flowers. Come on, let's go out there where she is," he answered.

Grandpa Jacob had limited use of his legs. Thomas saw that every step was a struggle for him. He mostly pulled his legs along one after the other as he made his way to the rear door. Despite the effort, Thomas couldn't help but notice the cheerfulness in his voice.

"We have visitors, Isabelle," Grandpa called out when he opened the door. Grandma Isabelle was down on her knees doing something with her flowers. She turned around to see Maria and Thomas standing with Grandpa Jacob.

"Oh, what a pleasant surprise," she said as she raised herself to her feet and walked over to where they were standing. She reached out her hand to Thomas. "You must be Thomas," she said.

"Yes, I am, Grandma Isabelle. I'm so happy to meet you," he said as he took her hand.

"Our grandson spoke highly of you in his letters. Let's go in and sit a while," she said as she motioned to the sunroom. "Grandpa and I can't stand upright for very long." They followed her to the porch where she kicked off her garden clogs and removed her apron and gloves. Then, they all headed to the sunroom and sat down.

It was a beautiful, sunny, fall morning. There was a slight chill in the air, but the temperature was rising quite steadily. The colorful leaves had just begun to fall from the trees. The fall foliage in the rear of their home was arrayed in many splendid colors. Looking out from the sunroom, one could tell that the landscape was meticulously cared for.

"Do you do all the work yourself?" Thomas asked, pointing to the yard.

"We used to before the accident. Now, Johnny comes by once a week to help out. Johnny's our yard man. We couldn't keep it looking this way without him."

"It's really gorgeous. I can see the tender loving care that has gone into it," Thomas said.

"Yes, that yard has brought many joyful memories. We used to rake the leaves in a pile and Maria and Allen would jump in them when they were little," Grandpa Jacob reminisced. Sighing, he looked at Thomas.

"Thomas, I wish we were meeting under different circumstances. Allen wrote us in his letters about you and the possibility of our meeting this way if he didn't make it back. We told him we looked forward to meeting you when both of you returned home safely from the war. Allen will truly be missed by his family and this community. It's hard for us to accept the reality that he won't be coming to see us anymore."

"How are you coping with the change that has occurred in your life?" Grandma Isabelle asked.

"Until recently, I haven't been handling things well at all. After I woke up in the hospital and realized what had happened, I was told that Allen hadn't survived his injury. It devastated me. For a long time, I was trapped in a state of anger and depression. I think about Allen every day. We only knew each other for a short period of time, but it seemed as if I had known him all of my life. We had so much in common. I thought for sure that we both would make it back alive. All of the plans that I made for myself included both of my legs. This has been extremely difficult for me to accept. I'm learning to cope with this new reality. Allen paid the ultimate price in this war and that truly is a tragedy," Thomas explained.

"We can identify with the sudden change that has occurred in your life. We both were blessed although the accident also changed our lives forever, that day. The car that we were traveling in was crushed and we were pinned in it for about an hour. The paramedics had to work on us in that position. When we reached the hospital, the doctors didn't know if either one of us would make it because of the loss of blood. Our church community sent up prayers for us. When we were released from the hospital, we didn't know if we could continue living in the privacy of our own home or if we would have to move into an assisted living facility. We learned to take it one day at a time and get the help we needed so we could determine what we could and could not do. In the beginning, we had to swallow a lot of pride and let people teach us how to do things differently," Grandma Isabelle said.

"I didn't think I would be able to drive again after the accident. I didn't know if I would have the courage to try. When something of this magnitude happens, most of us question the very foundation that we have built our lives on. I admit I had some reservations in that area myself. The things that helped us maintain our faith and belief in God were the love, care, and support of our family, friends, and neighbors and other people we didn't know who came to our aid and helped us learn to live independent lives again. We had to learn to do things differently. The van that we have is specially equipped for people who have lost the use of their legs. All of the controls are at hand level. Modern technology continues to move forward and some of the advances have helped people like me live productive lives. We have to take advantage of that. God is good all the time," Grandpa Jacob explained.

"I was afraid we were going to lose you both," Maria piped in. "It was a long road to your recovery. When Allen and I saw you in the hospital, we couldn't stop crying. There was nothing we could do. We felt so helpless. Allen suggested forming a prayer group with our friends. We started praying twice a day, once at 7:30 a.m. and again at 7:30 p.m. The group still exists today. Wherever we are at those chosen times, we say a prayer for the persons chosen for the week. The group has grown tremendously since its inception. Allen had the foresight to start that group. He's no longer with us, but that group continues to thrive and as you know, prayer is a powerful thing. So you see, good things can come from tragic situations. We have to keep an open mind and we have to learn to let go and let God direct our lives," Maria remarked.

"This has been a learning experience for me. Sitting here listening to you all, I realize this visit is to comfort and encourage all of us. It seems as if Allen planned this before leaving for the war. It is obvious to me that he prepared his soul for living even if he lost his life as we know it. Always keep your house in order, my mother always used to say. Now, I truly know its meaning. Allen knew this. For me, this visit is to teach me that my life is still worth living. He knew, if I listened to how you two overcame the difficulty you faced after your accident, somehow, I would find that same courage to continue on with my life. I want to thank you for being candid with me," Thomas said.

"How long will you be here with us?" Maria asked him.

"I'll be leaving for home tomorrow. I didn't plan for a long stay," Thomas answered.

"We certainly are glad you came to see us. We want you to consider us part of your extended family. You're welcome to visit us at anytime. Charlie called after the conversation you all had about Allen's death when you arrived. He recorded the conversation. We want to hear it, but we won't ask you to repeat it again. We'll listen to it with Charlie and Clair," Grandpa Jacob told Thomas.

Later that afternoon, Charlie and Clair called to see what was going on. They were involved in some business meetings and regretted not being there. They told Maria and Thomas they were looking forward to seeing them when they got home.

Grandma Isabelle and Maria went inside and made lunch and served it in the sunroom. They talked the afternoon away until it was time for Maria and Thomas to leave. Grandpa Jacob and Grandma Isabelle thanked Thomas once again for coming. Thomas had really enjoyed his visit with Grandpa Jacob and Grandma Isabelle. They both showed a zest for life despite the hardship life had placed on them.

"We wish you could visit with us longer, but we understand you have important things to do in order for you to get on with your life," Grandpa said.

"I can assure you, this will not be my last visit. I'll be back to see you once my leg is healed. This has been a healing experience for me. To meet such courageous people as yourselves is inspiring," he said, shaking Grandpa Jacob's hand. "When I woke up in the hospital and learned what happened, I was spiritually depleted. I was angry with everything and everyone. Since then, I have met some wonderful people of God. At first, I didn't want to hear what they were saying. I wanted my body to be as it was before going to war. Deep down, I knew it was impossible, but I was determined not to settle for anything less. I was holding God accountable for all that had happened to me and I didn't want to acknowledge that he was not to blame, but I had to. You see, I put myself in a no-win situation and there was only one way out. With the help of people like yourselves, I am surrendering to Christ, my Lord and Savior," Thomas reflected.

Before Thomas and Maria left for home, they all held hands and Grandpa Jacob said a prayer and asked God to continue to guide Thomas and give him the courage to face the difficulty that lay ahead of him.

When Thomas and Maria arrived at her home, her parents weren't there. Charles and Clair came in about an hour later. They anxiously inquired about what happened during the day at Grandpa's and Grandma's. After sharing the conversations of the day, Thomas told them he would be leaving the next morning. They wanted him to stay longer, but understood why he had to leave. They had supper and sat around talking until 10:30 p.m. The time seemed to pass rather quickly. They all said goodnight and retired to their bedrooms. Before Thomas got into bed, he called his parents to tell them what time his flight would arrive in Atlanta.

The next morning after breakfast, Thomas went back to his room and got his bag. The Jeffersons were extremely quiet as he walked back to where they were seated. He saw sadness on their faces, but there were no tears in their eyes.

"I would like to make a request of you, Mr. Jefferson. Would you mind taking me by to visit Allen's grave site on our way to the airport?" Thomas asked solemnly.

"Yes, I will be glad to stop. It's only a few minutes off the freeway. Did you know he was laid to rest in the national cemetery here?" Mr. Jefferson asked.

"No, I didn't know that."

"Do you mind if I come along with you?" Mrs. Jefferson asked Thomas as he started toward the car.

"No, of course not," he told her.

"I'm coming too," Maria said as she walked with them to the car.

FINAL SALUTE

On the way to the cemetery, there wasn't much conversation. The closer they got, the quieter they became. Thomas didn't want this visit to upset the family. He could tell it was difficult for them and he was feeling emotional himself. He knew he had to do this before returning home. He had to see Allen's final resting place.

When they drove onto the grounds of the cemetery, he noticed several visitors that were walking throughout the grounds. This was his first time visiting a national cemetery. He was impressed with how immaculate it was kept. It had a manicured lawn and the American Flag was displayed all over the grounds.

When Mr. Jefferson stopped the car, everyone got out and walked a short distance to Allen's grave site. It was a moving experience for Thomas and the family. When he focused on Allen's grave and the headstone in particular, there was a flood of emotion that came rushing to the surface. Thomas tried to fight it off, but he lost. He started weeping uncontrollably. The Jeffersons rushed to his aid. They were concerned he might lose his balance and fall. With tears in their eyes, they maintained their composure and assisted Thomas.

"Just let it all out, Thomas. You're going to be okay," Maria said as she patted his back.

"It'll get easier as time goes on," Mrs. Jefferson added.

"Coming here today will make it easier on you when you come back again," Mr. Jefferson replied.

"I thought I could control my emotions but I was wrong. I have never lost anyone with whom I had this close a relationship with before. I wonder how many times this particular scene has repeated itself throughout this cemetery. What we see here is a result of man's inhumanity to man throughout the world. I pray for the day when we, the people of the world, will be able to settle our differences without bloodshed," Thomas lamented. "The Bible speaks of a time when man will study war no more. I know it won't happen in my lifetime, but the world and its inhabitants will be able to experience the joy that peace can bring when it comes," Thomas said as he looked over the cemetery observing the visitors that day.

"I know if Allen was alive, he would agree with you. I have never been to war, but I have seen and experienced the result of it. At this stage of human consciousness, war is sometimes a necessary evil that man must perpetrate upon each other to foster freedom. That won't always be the case. In order for the rest of us to live in freedom, some have to make the ultimate sacrifice. No one wants it to be their loved one. When the call to war is heard deep within their souls, the brave ones go and they go willingly. The selection process of who will live and who will sacrifice their lives is totally out of human hands. I believe war should only be fought as a last resort after all negotiations have failed and an agreement cannot be reached. This cemetery and many like it all over the world are filled with the bones of our brave men and women who have given their lives in the name of freedom. I sincerely hope none were given in vain. If some were, we will never know, but God will make the final judgment if those in power have called our brave men and women to war unnecessarily. We must put our trust in him," Mr. Jefferson expounded.

"Are you okay now, Thomas?" Mrs. Jefferson asked. Thomas seemed to have regained his composure.

"Yes, I'm okay now. I just couldn't contain my emotions."

"We've all been there. It'll get better, you'll see," she said as she patted his hand.

"I'm ready to leave whenever you all are ready," Thomas said.

"I guess we better go so you can make your flight," Maria suggested. They all readied themselves and started toward the car. Thomas turned around and gave Allen a final salute before leaving. He had regained his composure and although he'd lost it, he'd felt relief while visiting the grave site.

When they arrived at the airport, Mr. Jefferson stopped the car at curbside. He and Thomas got out and Thomas said goodbye to Mrs. Jefferson and Maria while Mr. Jefferson popped the trunk to get his luggage. They both thanked him for coming and asked him to come back soon. He told him them that he would.

"You take good care of yourself and please stay in touch," Mr. Jefferson said.

"I will sir. I'm so glad I came to visit with you and your family. Tell Grandpa Jacob and Grandma Isabelle I said thanks for the encouragement. They are a remarkable couple and you and your family are just wonderful. I love you all," Thomas told Mr. Jefferson emotionally.

"We love you too, Thomas. Have a good flight," Mr. Jefferson responded. As the car pulled away, they waved goodbye to each other.

After boarding the plane, Thomas settled in for his flight home. One of the other passengers was reading a newspaper and Thomas could see the headline on the front page. It read, "War Protestors March on Washington, D.C." He turned his head and looked out over the wing of the plane, focusing on the clouds.

When the plane landed in Atlanta, most of his family was waiting at the gate to greet him. When he saw them, he smiled with a happiness that had been missing since the war. He hugged them all and told them he was glad they came to meet him.

On the way home, he told them about his experience with Allen's family. Thomas' attitude about life had changed. It was obvious to his parents and siblings. This visit had really made a difference in his life. When John drove into the yard of their home, Mack was lying on the front porch. He stood up with his tail wagging in anticipation. Thomas stepped out of the van and Mack walked over and rubbed his body against Thomas' leg. Thomas reached down and rubbed Mack on his back. Then, he went inside to put away his things and use the bathroom.

Later, after talking with his family, he went out in the yard and started playing with Mack. His siblings followed him out. John and Sarah stood on the porch and watched. Mack was having the time of his life. There were other challenges for Thomas on his road to recovery, but with God's help and the love and support of his family and friends, he became one of the most successful siblings in the Goodwin family.

MACK, THE FAMILY DOG

John had no way of knowing what a valuable friend Mack would become when he'd first seen him, early one morning, lying beside Baker's Ferry Road. John thought he was dead. Mack was suffering from several wounds that seemed to have been caused by a vehicle.

After looking him over carefully, John found that his heart was barely beating. He was alive, but he wouldn't be for long without medical attention. John put him in the back of his pickup truck and carried him to Friends of Animals, a local veterinarian group. Mack had two broken legs and internal bleeding. The veterinarian told John he probably wouldn't make it.

"I can save you some money if you let me put him down," he said.

"The dog isn't mine," John answered. "What are his chances of recovering?"

"About 50/50," the doctor informed him.

"They sound good to me. Try to save him."

"Okay, it's your money. What name should I put on his tag?"

"We'll call him Mack until we learn his real name."

"Mack it is," the doctor said as he got ready to try to save Mack's life.

John ran an ad in the local newspaper for the owner of the brown and white pit bull. He included his contact information and asked to be called at once. When there was no immediate reply, John thought Mack might have been abandoned. John placed another ad and elaborated that the dog had been injured and was in desperate need of medical care. He never received a response.

Mack slowly responded to the medical treatment. John visited him every other day. Mack's wounds healed and, as time passed, he and John became friends. When the doctor presented John with the bill, he didn't say a word. He simply pulled out his wallet and paid it.

"That's a lot of money," the doctor noted as John handed him the bills.

"A man must do what he believes is right no matter the cost," John quietly answered.

"Mr. Goodwin, you're a good man," the doctor told him as John and Mack left the clinic and headed home.

Sarah had never asked how much it cost and John had never told her. When John came home with Mack, he didn't know where he was going to put him. He had been so concerned about Mack's health that he had forgotten to build a doghouse. Sarah met him at the back door as he came in. Noticing the puzzled look on his face, she asked him what was wrong.

"I forgot to build a doghouse," he said.

"Bring him into the house until you build one," she said. "He isn't a mean dog, is he?"

"I don't think he is. He's never behaved that way toward me," John said as he carried Mack into the house. He noticed some covers on the floor in the corner near the fireplace. He looked questioningly at Sarah.

"You can put him there," she replied, suddenly feeling shy in face of his scrutiny.

"You knew I had no place to put him, didn't you?"

"Yes," she said as she shook her head. "John, you're a good man, but you can't think of everything. That's why God created women for you men."

"I suppose you're right," he laughed. "I sure thank him for mine."

He laid Mack down and then grabbed her and planted a big kiss on her cheek. "Thanks, Sarah," he said. "Mack needs to be inside until he's healed completely."

"Is he house trained?" Sarah asked.

"I don't really know. I have a feeling we'll know by morning."

John awoke about 1:00 a.m. to check on Mack. He was sound asleep in the corner, lying very still. When he heard John, he woke up and began barking.

"What's wrong, boy?" John asked. He kneeled down and began patting and rubbing Mack, but that didn't quiet him. John looked at Mack.

"Are you hungry?" he asked. Mack kept barking. Sarah came down.

"John, what's wrong?"

"I don't know," he told her. John looked back at Mack and saw him standing on his feet. He was slowly moving toward the door. He looked at John and Sarah. They had no idea what was wrong with him. John realized that there was a lot he didn't know about Mack. Maybe it just wasn't safe to have him in their home. Then it finally occurred to John that Mack was trying to tell him he had to go outside. John walked over and opened the door. After Mack finished his business, he came back inside, laid down, and went to sleep.

The weeks passed by slowly. John never built the doghouse. He bathed Mack every week and Mack stayed in the corner.

They had a cat named Dude who was very finicky. Dude really belonged to Sarah. John liked him, but he wasn't really a cat person. When Dude saw Mack for the first time, he didn't like the dog at all. Dude thought he was king of the house. He didn't like the mongrel dog infringing on his domain. After all, he had marked everything with his scent. This dog was fouling things up.

When Mack fully recovered, he went just about everywhere with John. There were times when John left Mack at home while he attended church. Later, he'd find him waiting outside the church for him when service was over.

Mack didn't like riding on the back of the truck. Instead, he ran alongside it. Of course, he couldn't keep up with the truck if John didn't want him to. John really got a kick out of seeing Mack run. Sometimes, John enjoyed racing with Mack on the way home. Other times, they took it nice and slow.

Mack loved to aggravate the farm animals. He was always in some kind of mischief. The cows often chased him, but he was too fast for them to catch. They chased him anyway and he loved every minute of it.

Mack and Dude had many confrontations around the farm. They just naturally didn't like each other. Dude was usually the instigator.

One day, a strange dog attacked Dude as he walked across the backyard. Mack was with John who was feeding the cows when he heard a dog barking. The dog had Dude on the ground and wouldn't let him go. When Mack heard the commotion, he ran toward the house. Alarmed, John stopped what he was doing and followed in the truck.

When Mack reached the house, Dude was a bloody mess. Sarah had tried to stop the dog, but she was afraid to get too close. Mack caught the dog around the neck. The dog had been so focused on Dude that he hadn't seen Mack coming. The dog let go of Dude and Mack fought him for what seemed like a long time. It was a vicious fight. The dog finally broke free of Mack's grip and turned and ran out of the yard with Mack in hot pursuit. He went down the road as fast as he could. He couldn't beat Mack fighting, but he could run faster. Mack chased him until he was out of sight. Lucky for the dog, Mack never saw him again.

John and Sarah carried Dude to the veterinarian. Dude looked worse than he was. After examining him, the vet assured them that Dude would be his old self in about two weeks.

"By the way, Mr. Goodwin, what happened to Mack?" the doctor asked.

"He's still with us. I couldn't find his owner. You know, old Mack saved Dude's life today."

"Does this cat belong to you or did you find him along the road also?"

"We've had him since he was a kitten," John said.

Dude recovered from his wounds and began walking around, just as territorial as ever. If Dude had been able to talk and tell it straight, he would have said he had been a happy cat to see Mack coming to his rescue.

One morning, about six months later, a man knocked on John and Sarah's front door.

"Who can that be?" John asked. "Are you expecting anyone, Sarah?"

"No, I'm not," she replied. John went to open the door and saw a man with a leash in his hand.

"Good morning, can I help you?"

"I came for the dog," the man replied. Surprised, John asked him what dog he was referring to.

"The one you call Mack," the man told him impatiently.

"Is he your dog?" John asked.

"Yes, he is," the man replied. "I'll be taking him now."

"Just a minute, sir. Could you describe your dog for me," John asked.

"I really don't think this is necessary, but I'll satisfy your curiosity. He's a brown pit bull with a white chest and paws."

"John wasn't going to let Mack go so easily. "Do you have any papers to prove your ownership?" he countered.

"No I do not," the man said testily, "but the dog is mine. Let me ask you a question," he said to John. "Does the dog belong to you?"

"No, he doesn't," John said. "From what you've told me, I'm not sure he belongs to you either. You go get the papers and maybe you can take the dog, Mr…"

"My name is Bass, Big Joe Bass I'm called by some," the man interrupted.

"Well, I'm John Goodwin."

"Mr. Goodwin, I'll be back tomorrow. You can count on it," the man said as he stomped off.

John knew he had upset the man, but he had become too attached to Mack to give him to someone who might not be his owner. The man's name sounded familiar to John so he called some of his neighbors and asked if they had ever heard of him. None of them recognized his name or knew anything about him.

John went back to his daily activities and didn't think much about it until that evening. One of the local television stations was doing a report on illegal dog fighting. They were showing two dogs fighting in a pit when John realized that one of the dogs looked like Mack. The news reporter called the dog "Spike, The Canine Killer". The reporter stated that Spike was the most vicious of them all. He had nine confirmed kills to his credit. That really got John's attention. He looked as closely as he could, but he wasn't sure whether the dog was Mack.

John couldn't believe this could be the same dog he'd seen on the evening news. When the evening news was over, John went outside to see Mack. When Mack saw John, he immediately ran over to him with his tail wagging madly. He was always happy to see John.

Joe Bass returned the next morning with a bill of sale. He demanded that John release Mack to him immediately. Mack was like a member of Johns' family and he didn't want to see him go. John was greatly disappointed, but he realized that he had to release Mack to Joe Bass.

"Where's the dog?" Joe Bass demanded.

When Mack saw John, he started jumping and wagging his tail. Mack's demeanor changed when he saw Joe Bass. He began growling and assumed a defensive stance. Mack definitely didn't like Joe Bass.

"I don't know what's wrong with the dog," Joe Bass replied. "He has never acted this way before. Maybe he doesn't remember me."

"Maybe he remembers you too well," John said pointedly.

"Will you please put this leash on him and put him on the back of my truck?" Joe Bass asked. When John just stared back at him, he said "he's my dog and I have a legal right to him."

John reluctantly took the leash and put it on Mack. Despite his whimpering, John led Mack to Joe Bass' truck and put him on the back. It tore him up inside to do this, especially when Mack looked him in the eyes. As he tied the leash, Joe Bass started the truck. John watched Mack as Joe Bass drove out of sight. When he looked around, he saw Sarah standing in the door, tears rolling down her face.

The next couple of days were very lonely for John. On the third day, he was feeding his cows and other livestock when it suddenly dawned on him what had happened. The reason Mack didn't want to go with Joe Bass was probably because of past experiences. 'I bet Mack is "Spike, The Canine Killer" and Joe Bass is his handler,' John thought to himself. John knew he had put Mack's life in danger. He decided to go talk to the local sheriff.

The sheriff ran a check on Joe Bass and anyone else associated with dog fighting. Joe Bass' name was one of several that came back as confirmed dog handlers and trainers. He was wanted in several states for organizing and staging these fights.

"Do you know where they were headed?" the sheriff asked.

"I don't know," John responded.

"You can bet he's organizing another dog fight. It also says here that these dogs have a short life span due to the severe wounds they receive during the fights. This dog Mack that you told me about, if he's "Spike, The Canine Killer", I understand why Joe Bass wanted him back. He's a very profitable dog. If for any reason he should show up at your home again, please let me know immediately."

"Why didn't I check with the sheriff before I let Joe Bass take Mack away. Sometimes, John Goodwin, you do some stupid things," John muttered to himself. "Sooner or later, Mack will be killed in one of those fights. I'm sorry, old friend," John said tearfully.

John never heard anything about an upcoming dogfight or one that had recently taken place. He knew the fights were kept secret because they were illegal. John came to the conclusion that he'd done everything he could at the time Mack was taken. He had to get on with his life.

Early one morning, about two months later, John was on his way to feed the livestock. He closed the back door behind him and he saw Mack lying near the barn. It surprised him. There was something strange about him.

When Mack saw John he just stared at him. He didn't make a sound. John didn't know if he should go to him or stay away. He decided to let him be for a while. He went back inside and brought out some food and water for Mack. He then went inside and told Sarah that Mack was back and he was acting strange.

"Did you give him some food and water?" she asked.

"Yes, I did, but he isn't eating or drinking."

"Don't worry," Sarah said, "he will when he's hungry."

"He's acting as if he doesn't know me."

"Maybe he doesn't trust you now," she said. "He remembers you putting him on the back of that truck. I wonder where he came from."

John watched Mack from the window. Mack got to his feet slowly.

"Oh, my God! What happened to you, Mack?" John exclaimed as he contemplated going closer to Mack. He had been injured and could barely walk. He had blood on him from wounds on his right side, his back, and around his neck. He just barely made it to the food and water. John knew he had to do something to help him.

Mack began to eat a little bit. When he finished eating, John went outside to see if Mack would let him get close enough to see how severe his wounds were. When the door opened, Mack got to his feet and started to growl. John stopped in his tracks. He knew he had to regain Mack's confidence. The only way he could do it was to risk being hurt himself. He moved forward, telling Mack he was not going to hurt him. Mack continued to growl, baring his teeth. John moved very slowly. When he got close enough to touch Mack he realized he was injured very badly.

John went back inside and got his first aid kit so he could tend to Mack's wounds. He heard a vehicle stop in his front yard. 'Who could that be?' he wondered.

"That might be Joe Bass," Sarah worried.

John walked around to the front yard and saw Joe Bass standing on the front porch poised to ring the doorbell.

"What are you doing here, Mr. Bass?" John asked.

"Have you seen Mack?" he asked. "He ran away a few days ago."

"You mean Spike, don't you, Mr. Bass?" John questioned pointedly.

"I don't have to answer that," he said.

"How did he get those wounds, Mr. Bass?" Sarah asked, standing in the doorway behind John.

"So, he is here," Joe replied. He walked around to the rear of the house looking for Mack, fully intending to take the dog with him.

"He got those wounds from fights he's been in since he left here, didn't he?" John asked.

"I told you, I don't have to answer any of your questions, Mr. Goodwin!" Joe Bass yelled.

"No, you don't have to answer any of my questions, Mr. Bass, but you will have to answer the sheriff's questions when he gets here. Maybe you can explain why there are several outstanding warrants for your arrest, in different states, for organizing and staging illegal dogfights."

"I'm going to take my dog. He had no right to come back here," Joe Bass said as he moved toward Mack.

"This dog has the right to live a good life free of hate and violence just like you and I do, Mr. Bass. I was asked to call the sheriff's office if you came here again. Sarah, go and make that call," John said. "Mr. Bass, you have about fifteen or twenty minutes before he arrives. I suggest you make good use of it."

Mack was carrying on something fierce. He was showing his hatred for Joe Bass.

"I don't ever want you to come to my home again. Mack is going to live the rest of his days in peace. Do I make myself clear?" John said as he placed himself between Mack and Joe Bass.

"I'm leaving," Joe Bass said as he headed toward his truck. He got in and drove away as fast as he could.

John and Sarah tended to Mack's wounds. He never growled at John again. They took him to the vet to get him proper care. In a few weeks, he was like his old self again. John heard that Joe Bass was arrested in Alabama a couple of weeks later for staging a dogfight.

THE FARM'S FORECLOSURE

"You know, we've been through some tough times during our marriage," John told Sarah as they continued looking through their photo albums.

"Yes, we have John, but they didn't last for long. When I look through the picture albums, I'm reminded of the good times more than the bad. I see a family that has overcome adversities and become stronger. We're always going to have problems in our lives. We live in an imperfect world, but it's always helpful to reflect back to where we started from to really understand how blessed we are. With the Lord's help, we were able to care for our family with the money the farm produced. This farm helped put the children through college. That's truly a blessing," she said with a smile.

"I never had the opportunity to finish school," John reflected. "I wanted to go to school, but I couldn't. I used to hear other kids talking about the things they were learning and I felt so bad. I started working on the farm with my father when I was eight years old. There wasn't any time for schooling. We worked from dawn to dusk. I learned to read and write by an oil lamp. My father died when I was fifteen years old and, since I was the oldest of four children, I had to become the man in the family. While other children my age were going to school, I had to work as a sharecropper to help feed the family. My daddy taught me how to produce good crops. He knew the process and what it takes to bring crops to harvest. He told me that if I do everything right and God doesn't send the rain, the plants won't produce. He said it takes a lot of faith and a deep belief in God to become a good farmer. Just before he died, he told me the rain might not come when you want it to, but most of the time, it will come when you need it. You must be patient and wait. Sarah, I know you've heard the story many times. I didn't mean to ramble on like that," John said thinking how tired Sarah must be.

"I never get bored hearing about your life," Sarah told him with a twinkle in her eye. "You were not able to go to school but you were able to send our children to college because your father taught you the one thing he knew how to do well. He taught you how to become a successful farmer. When you were eight years old, you didn't realize you would own this farm one day. We can't see into the future. We have to do the best we can with what we have at the present time," Sarah said.

"Sarah, I believe you missed your calling. You should have been a counselor," John told her.

John continued looking through the family picture albums. He could see his family had truly been blessed over the years. All eight of his children were alive and well.

"We can discuss our finances tomorrow. I think I'll get ready for bed," John told her. While John was taking a shower, he was reminded of one of the things his father used to say when things were not going well.

"The Earth belongs to God and the fullness thereof. He only shares it with us while we are here."

After saying his prayers, John got in the bed and fell asleep. Sarah woke him up just after midnight. She was so excited.

"What's wrong?" he asked.

"Listen, John, do you hear it?" John heard thunder in the distance as rain began pelting the rooftop.

"God is sending his precious rain," Sarah said.

"Yes, he is. The rain is here!" John exclaimed as he hopped out of bed and looked out the window. Sarah couldn't help but smile as he danced around excitedly.

The next morning, John checked the fields. They were improving tremendously. The plants were straightening up. He thought he might have a chance if the rain continued for a while. He wanted to make enough on the crop to pay back the loan.

When John came home, Sarah wanted to know how the fields were looking.

"They're fifty percent better than yesterday. We might be able to pay off most, if not all of the loan if it continues to rain."

The next day, John decided to go to the bank and talk with his loan officer. He explained his concern over the condition of his fields. He was afraid he might not make enough on the sale of his crops to pay the loan. The loan officer assured him that he understood the situation.

"We will take a look at everything when the harvest is in. I will make a recommendation to the loan committee. I'm sure everything will be worked out satisfactorily for both parties," the officer assured him.

John went home and talked everything over with Sarah. They both agreed the only thing they could do was pray that the rain continue. When the harvest came in, they agreed they'd go to the bank and try to work everything out if they didn't make enough to pay back the loan.

The rain continued to come, but it was too late for John to have the type of harvest he needed to pay the loan in full. After the crops were harvested and sold, John added up all the money he had received. The total came to exactly $16, 212.10. His note at the bank was $37, 521.15. He was $21, 309.05 short of paying it off. He took every cent to his loan officer and showed him every receipt and check that he'd received. The loan officer said he would go over everything and would make a recommendation to the loan committee. He asked John to check back with him on Wednesday of the next week.

"I should have some good news for you," he said. John thanked him and promised to return the next Wednesday.

Waiting for Wednesday to come seemed like an eternity. Early Wednesday morning, John went back to the bank alone. He didn't see his loan officer at the desk where he usually sat. There was someone else there. When he inquired about him, he was told the officer no longer worked at the bank.

"Was he your loan officer?" he was asked.

"Yes, he was," John said.

"I'll be handling his loans from now on. Sir, what is your name?"

"My name is John Goodwin."

"My name is Ron Harper," the man said as he gave John a brief handshake. "Have a seat, Mr. Goodwin. I'll be right with you."

When Mr. Harper returned to his desk, John asked him what the loan committee had decided. The decision came as a shock to John.

The loan officer told John the loan committee understood the dilemma he and other farmers had for the last couple of years.

"The previous loan officer recommended your loan be extended with enough money to put in your crops for next year. However, the loan committee didn't agree. The bank officials are afraid if too many farmers default on their loans, they will put the bank in a very unstable position. I'm sorry to inform you of the bank's decision to foreclose your loan. If the total outstanding amount on your loan is not paid in full, the bank will have to seize your assets."

John felt like he was about to have a heart attack when he heard those words. It took him a few long minutes to regain his composure.

"How can they do this to me? I've been banking here all of my life. I've been in this situation before and I have always paid the bank everything I owed them. This time will be no different," John explained. "I want the loan committee to reconsider their decision," he requested.

"I'm afraid the decision is final Mr. Goodwin."

"This ain't right," he told Mr. Harper angrily.

"I'm sorry, Mr. Goodwin, it's out of my hands. The only way to save your farm is to come up with all of the money."

"How long do I have before the bank starts the proceedings?" John asked.

"About two weeks," Mr. Harper's voice rang out like a death sentence.

John was devastated. He drove home in a daze. How could he tell Sarah about the foreclosure on their property? He stopped off at the fishing pond. He was trying to decide if he was going to tell Sarah or wait and try to work everything out himself. He didn't want to upset her or make her unhappy. John decided to wait before telling her. He had an old friend who might be able to help him out. He'd try to get the money from him.

When John arrived home, Sarah was making dinner.

"How did everything go at the bank?" she asked. John was about to tell the biggest lie of his life.

"Everything went just fine," he said as he looked into her eyes. "The bank extended our loan with enough additional money to put in the crops for next year."

"I told you everything was going to work out okay," she said with a huge grin on her face.

'Please forgive me, Lord,' John thought to himself. He just couldn't tell her the truth.

John knew two people he thought he could get the money from. One was Tommie Banks, an old friend who was financially well off due to some stocks he'd invested in years ago. He had always told John if he could ever help him to let him know. John called Tommie Banks the next morning to arrange a time to meet with him. Tommie's wife told John that Tommie was out of town and wouldn't return until the next Monday. She told John she would ask Tommie to give him a call when she spoke with him. John thanked her and hung up. Tommie called back the next day.

"How are you, John?" he asked. John didn't kid around. He got straight to the point. He told Tommie about the pending foreclosure on his farm.

"I need $21, 309.05 to save my property. Will you let me have the money?"

"John, that's a lot of money," he said. "What kind of collateral do you have to guarantee my money?" Tommie asked.

"You have my word. I'll repay every cent. After I pay the bank, I'll give you the deed to my property until the loan is paid in full."

Tommie told John that was good enough for him. He told John it would take about a week to get the money. He had to pull it out of some investments he had.

"You don't have to worry about the money, I'll let you have it," Tommie told John.

"Thanks Tommie, you don't know how much I appreciate this. I would like to keep this between us. I haven't told Sarah."

"I won't tell anyone but my wife. She has to know. She helps me handle our investments."

"I understand," John told him.

When John hung the phone up, he was in high spirits. He had his problem solved. All he had to do was wait for Tommie to get the money. John had known Tommie all his life. Unlike John, Tommie graduated from high school and earned an undergraduate degree in business. Their fathers were very close friends. Although they grew up together, they drifted apart after Tommie received his degree from college. John didn't feel comfortable being around Tommie and his friends because he didn't have much education.

Tommie didn't call John on Monday. John thought he was probably settling in from his trip. He decided to give him a couple of days before he gave him a call. Two days passed and he still hadn't heard from Tommie. On Thursday morning, John decided to call. He was told that Tommie wasn't in. His wife told John that she would have Tommie return his call as soon as possible.

Friday morning, Tommie called John and told him he had a delay in getting the money. He assured John he would have the money in two days.

John went to see his loan officer the next morning to see if he could get a delay on the foreclosure proceedings for a couple of days. When John arrived at the bank, he sat down and waited on his loan officer. When the loan officer came out of his office, he was with Tommie Banks. They were both smiling. They didn't see John, but he saw them. He started to approach Tommie, but decided not to. He was sure that Tommie was there to get the money and that he would probably hear from Tommie later that evening.

When John met with the loan officer, he asked for a couple of days extension before the bank proceeded with further action.

"I'm sorry sir. The foreclosure proceeding was taken on the 17th of this month," the loan officer informed him. John's mouth dropped open.

"Sir, I was in here on the 16th and you told me that I had two weeks before any action would be taken," John told him in disbelief.

"I was wrong," the loan officer stated matter-of-factly. "It's totally out of my hands. I'm sorry. From what I've heard, the sheriff will be out to your farm in about two days to seize your assets."

John was so shaken, he could barely walk back to his truck. He had never been in this position before. Tears rolled down his face as he drove home. He had to stop his truck until he regained his composure.

"How could I let this happen?" he asked himself. "I should have told Sarah."

After he got home, he called Tommie Banks. His wife told him that Tommie was out of town. John knew she was lying. He had just seen him about two hours earlier at the bank.

John called Fred Freeman who owned a finance company and made loans with much higher interest rates than the bank. John was told he was out of town on vacation and wouldn't be back for seven days. John was disgusted! Nothing seemed to work for him!

Tommie Banks never called John again. John was so frustrated that he couldn't think clearly. He decided to take matters into his own hands. 'No one is going to seize the property we've worked so hard for,' he thought. 'Just because we've had a couple of bad years, don't all the good years count for something? I'll stop them if I have to use force.'

On Sunday morning, John took his shotgun, his rifle, and a .45 caliber pistol to the barn. He was careful not to let Sarah see him. He methodically cleaned each of the weapons as he prepared for battle.

Sarah knew something was wrong. John was not his usual self. He was moody and distant. Frankly, he was worrying her.

"John, is there something wrong? Do you want to talk about it?" she asked when John came in for breakfast. "No, Sarah, everything is going to be just fine," he said distantly.

John returned to the barn with ammunition for the weapons. He stored the weapons and ammunition under some hay. Despite his preparations, John didn't sleep well that night. He tossed and turned with visions of battling the sheriff for his farm.

"What's wrong?" Sarah asked him after his tossing woke her up for the second time.

"I don't feel very well," John said evasively.

"Can I get you something to take?"

"You can get me a couple of aspirin, if you like," he replied. Even though John knew what he was planning to do the next day if the sheriff came to seize their property, he still couldn't tell Sarah the truth.

Early Monday morning, John got out of bed before Sarah. He made coffee and took a cup with him to the barn. He took the weapons and ammunition from beneath the hay and walked to the front of the house. He put the rifle on the right side of the house and the shotgun on the left side. He put the pistol in his pocket and took a seat on the front porch. John was not thinking clearly. Desperation had made him crazy.

In the distance, John could see dust rising as several cars were coming down the road toward his home. Behind the cars was a tractor-trailer truck. John's heart started pounding. He was so nervous he was having trouble standing.

"Oh my God, here they come," he said. As the cars came closer, John stood with his hands in his pockets. He broke out into a sweat.

When the cars turned into the driveway, John started down the steps. Halfway down, his legs gave way. He fell to the ground holding his chest and calling to Sarah. He lay there, semiconscious. He could barely hear Sarah when she asked him what was wrong.

"My heart," he whispered. "I'm sorry for the way things have turned out, Sarah," he said as he lost consciousness.

John was unconscious for seven days. He was trapped in the darkness trying to find a way out. He could hear, but he couldn't make out what was going on around him. John lay there, unmoving as his family watched helplessly and prayed for him to regain consciousness. When he finally did, he saw Sarah sitting in a chair in the shadows.

"Hi princess," he said.

"Welcome back, John," she said as she stood to call for the doctor.

"I'm sorry about everything," he whispered.

"John, we're not going to talk about anything other than your health. We'll discuss other matters when you're well."

When the doctor arrived, he told Sarah she would have to leave until he finished examining John. Before she left, she told John that everything was just fine.

He wondered how everything could be just fine when they had lost everything. Despite his despair, John's condition slowly improved. He and his family were able to have longer visits, but the doctor told his family not to talk about the farm or any other business matters until he was discharged from the hospital. Every time John tried to bring up a conversation about the farm, his family would tell him they were not going to talk about business. The only thing that mattered was for him to regain his health and strength. They refused to discuss anything else. Sarah smiled each time she reminded him of this. John couldn't understand how she could smile after losing everything.

On the day John was discharged, Sarah, John Jr., Thomas, and Rebecca were there to help put him into John Jr.'s van. When John Jr. got into the van and started out of the parking lot, John asked Sarah where they were going to stay.

"I'm sorry for losing the farm, Sarah" he told her.

"Dad, we're taking you home," John Jr. explained.

"You mean the farm?"

"Yes, honey. He means the farm," Sarah answered.

"How can that be? Just before I fell, I saw the people come into our driveway to seize our property."

"Is that the reason you had the pistol in your back pocket?" she asked.

"Yes," he said as he averted his eyes in shame. "I know it was a stupid thing to do."

"John Goodwin, you could have gotten yourself killed! Nothing is worth your life. We can start over if we have to. We could never bring you back," Sarah fussed.

"Dad, the people you saw turning into the driveway were us. We were coming to tell you that the loan at the bank was paid off. We were bringing you the deed. You collapsed before we got close enough for you to recognize us," John Jr. explained.

"Wasn't there a tractor-trailer behind you?" John asked.

"Yes, there was. It continued down the road. It never turned into the driveway."

"John Jr., how did you all find out about the mess I made of everything? I never told anyone in the family, not even your mother."

"Daddy, you and mother always taught us that the Lord works in mysterious ways," Rebecca said. "The first loan officer you had was Paul Adams, right?"

"Yeah," John confirmed.

"I went to college with Felicia Adams, Paul's sister. After college, we drifted apart and I hadn't talked with her for about six months. A few days ago, I had this strange dream. In my dream, we were talking and she kept telling me she had something important to tell me. Every time I would ask her what it was, she would say to please call her. I asked her why she couldn't tell me then, but she kept saying to call her. When I woke up, I was saying those very words, please call me. That evening after work, I called her. I told her about the dream and we both cracked up about it. Somehow we started talking about her brother, Paul. She said that he was having a tough time keeping a job. He was laid off recently from a bank job that he had. I asked her what bank and she named the bank and told me where it was located. She said he told her the reason the bank let him go was because he didn't recommend foreclosure on more of his delinquent loans. She said the last loan he handled was for a farmer named Goodwin and he was trying to help the farmer with the loan. The president of the bank told him that he was too lenient with his accounts and laid him off. He wanted to help the farmers and the bank wanted to foreclose as many as they could because most of them had a lot of equity. He told her a man named Banks, who was supposed to be a friend of the farmer, came in before he left and tried to purchase the note. I realized that was the message God wanted her to give to me. I didn't tell her the last account Paul worked on was our farm. When I get back, I'm going to call her and explain all of this. It's going to knock her socks off! The reason Tommie didn't get it was because you had also put John Jr.'s name is also on the deed. We all got together and paid it off. Your deed is waiting for you at home."

"John, you should have told me. Don't keep things from me just because you think I'll be upset or hurt. Our marriage vows were for better or worse, in sickness and in health. I'm your wife, you can tell me anything," Sarah put in.

"Sarah, I know you're right. Everything happened so fast, I couldn't think straight. I thought I had it all worked out. It's a sad day when you can't trust your friends. Tommie knew all along he wasn't going to let me have the money."

"Yeah, he knew," Thomas agreed, "but dad, you always said things have a way of working themselves out, if you believe."

When they got home, there was a banner across the driveway. It read "WELCOME HOME DADDY!" They stopped the van and Robert, Terry, Jimmie, Melanie, and Mary came out to greet them. John was still a little weak, but he was so excited to see his children and to return home. He had never thought things would turn out this way. He thought he had lost it all. It had never occurred to him to ask his children for help. He sat down in his favorite chair as his children presented him with his deed of ownership. John was a very happy man.

"You children don't know how much I appreciate this. You saved the place," he said emotionally.

"Dad, we're family and that's what a family is supposed to do," Rebecca answered.

"Mom and dad, we could never repay you for the things you've done for us, but we can help make life a little easier for you in your golden years," Robert said.

"This is a check for ten thousand dollars to use as you will. Don't try to talk us out of doing this, we've already put this amount aside for you," Terry explained. "Maybe next year will be a better year for the farm."

"The Lord sure has been good to us as a family," Sarah sighed.

"Yes, he has," John agreed as he accepted the check.

John looked over at his rifle, shotgun, and pistol in the gun cabinet. 'I could have done a terrible thing,' he thought to himself.

"Dad, do you think you would like to go fishing with us when you're feeling better?" Thomas asked.

"I sure would," he answered. "How are all the grandchildren?"

"They're doing just fine. We decided to leave them at home. We thought they might be too much for you this trip. We'll all be together on Thanksgiving," Mary said.

"I'm really looking forward to that," John replied as he thought of his grandchildren.

At the dinner table that evening, John led the family in prayer. He blessed the food and thanked the Lord for his family. He realized just how rich his life had been. He wouldn't take any amount of money in exchange for what he had.

When everyone went to bed for the night, Sarah told John that she loved him too much to have come so close to losing him. She told him that he shouldn't try to shoulder all of the responsibility alone.

"I love you too, Sarah" he told her. "I guess I'm set in my ways and I need to make a change. I have always tried to protect my family because that's what I thought a man should do. The children are grown. Maybe we need to consider selling part of the farm so we will have enough money to live on. I don't know if I'll be able to work the farm again."

"We'll talk more about it tomorrow, John," she replied. "Good night my prince."

"Good night princess," John said as he kissed her goodnight.

The next morning, after breakfast, John asked his family to join him and Sarah in the family room. John told the family that he and Sarah had been thinking about their future.

"Your mother and I talked briefly last night about the possibility of selling part of the farm to free up some cash so we could have something to live on. What you have done to save the farm is just wonderful. We also realize that you can't continue to support us financially for the rest of our lives. You have your own families and responsibilities. I would rather sell part of the farm than risk losing it year after year. Your mother and I aren't getting any younger. I want your opinions, but first I want Sarah to tell us how she feels."

Sarah took a moment to think. "John, I really don't know what is best for us right now," she answered. "I do know that we must prepare for the days when we won't be able to work the farm. I have loved this farm ever since I first saw it. I hate the idea of parting with any of it. After what we've just gone through,

I don't want us to be in that position again though. Selling part is better than losing it all," Sarah said.

"John, Jr., what do you think?" John asked while looking at his oldest child.

"Dad, I want us to do what's best for you and mom. Sitting here listening, I realize you have given this a lot of thought. I agree with mom. I know God doesn't want us to become too attached to material things, but I really love this farm." His siblings nodded in agreement. "I know you are getting older," he continued, "and you might not be able to work the farm again with your heart condition. Age is going to slow all of us down. There is a decision that has to be made, but I'm not sure what it should be. Selling part is better than risking it all, year after year. Until we decide what to do, please let us know if you need any financial help. Don't let your pride get in your way, dad. If you taught us anything, you taught us that our blessings come from helping others in need. If we had not received the love and guidance you gave, we wouldn't be who we are today."

"This farm gave me my life back," Thomas interjected. "I often think of the time I spent with Mack near the pond when I came back from the war. This farm didn't just grow crops, but it also grew us as a family. Land was made to grow things. None of us has any intention of returning to farm this land, but I would love to see it continue to produce crops. I know mom and dad aren't physically able to do it anymore. Maybe we could find a young couple who love farming and would like to take a chance on this farm. That way, dad could share the extensive knowledge he has obtained over the years."

"Don't forget, I have a lot of knowledge of farming also," Sarah chimed in.

"Thomas, that's an excellent idea," John agreed excitedly.

"All of this gives us a lot to think about. Mom and dad, I believe it could work if we find the right couple. The weather isn't going to continue this way forever. This drought is going to end. Dad, you have all the tools and machinery to operate the farm. The only thing they would need is enough money to put in the first crop."

"Maybe we do need some new blood to get this farm going again. I think it would be a great opportunity for some ambitious couple," John posed.

"John, I believe you're sold on Thomas' idea," Sarah mused.

"Sarah, you have always known I love to farm. I love to smell a freshly plowed field. I would love to see someone continue farming this land. It has been good to us, but maybe it's time we share it with someone else."

Everyone thought it was a great idea, but there was no firm decision made. They decided to think about everything that was discussed and they would try to make a decision at Thanksgiving.

"When are you all leaving?" John asked. "I don't want to see you go, but I know you can't stay forever."

"Tomorrow," was the consensus. They'd been home to make sure John was settled long enough. They had to get back to see how their families were doing.

"I guess I'd better enjoy you today then," John responded.

Sarah fell asleep holding John's hand that night. Somewhere, in the mystical world of dreams, a man with no face appeared as he had many times before.

As a child, Sarah had suffered with nightmares of a man with no face coming toward her. The only thing she could see was his hands. The nightmares had stopped when she was about ten years old. She remembered sitting in bed crying. Each time her mother would come in and comfort her.

Sarah's mother had been divorced from her father when she was eight years old. Afer the divorce, her mother went to work in a local grocery store. Providing a decent standard of living on the salary she earned proved to be very difficult. Sarah's mom was a hard-working woman and she loved her independence. She hadn't wanted to give it up, but she couldn't afford to maintain a place of her own. Eventually, they moved in with Sarah's aunt.

Sarah noticed a change in her mother's attitude just before they moved. Her mother had explained that things were going to be different.

"We won't be in our own home anymore. We'll be sharing Aunt Lillian's home. You must be careful not to break anything and always be polite," her mother had warned her.

"Mom, I love Aunt Lillian. I won't break any of her pretty things. She's so nice," Sarah gushed.

Aunt Lillian was an independent woman who was not afraid to speak her mind. Sarah had often stayed with her when she was a child. After Sarah and her mom, Ruth, moved in with Aunt Lillian, Ruth started working another part-time job to help pay her share of the monthly expenses. Aunt Lillian worked from home so she was there when Sarah came home from school every day. When Sarah got off of the bus, Aunt Lillian would be there waiting for her. As Sarah remembered, Aunt Lillian had been very happy to see Sarah get off the bus.

Aunt Lillian and Sarah spent a lot of time together. Every Friday after school, they would go to the Dairy Queen and have dessert. She told Sarah that after a hard week of work, everyone needed to celebrate a little.

The only job Ruth had been able to find to fit her schedule was working as a waitress in a bar at a hotel. She hadn't wanted to take the job, but it was the only one available. Ruth had wanted to earn enough money to afford a home of her own.

In the middle of the night, the nightmare intensified. Sarah began to toss and turn. She began mumbling. John heard her mumbling and woke up. He started calling Sarah's name and trying to shake her awake.

The room was filled with darkness. When Sarah awakened, she started crying and fighting John away.

"Honey! Honey! It's me, John" he called to her.

"No, no, get away," she screamed.

"Sarah, you have had a bad dream," he explained as she woke up. She seemed to calm down. She apologized to John as she held him tight and told him about the nightmare. 'It has returned, after all these years' she thought.

John was very concerned. He had never seen Sarah so emotional.

"John, can we leave the light on? I don't want to be in the dark," she asked.

"Sure, if that will help you through the night," he replied, worried about his wife.

The next morning, after breakfast, their children began packing and preparing to leave. John was up and around talking with everyone. Sarah was having a great time as if nothing had happened the night before. She assumed that none of the children had heard what occurred during the night. No one had mentioned anything to her. She thought they had all been so exhausted from the recent events that they had been sound asleep.

After the children left for the airport, John noticed Sarah's calm demeanor, but he wasn't fooled. He knew the nightmare was bothering her.

"Are you scared?" he asked her.

"No, I'm not scared, but John, when you recover, I'm going to visit Aunt Lillian."

"Do you want me to go with you?" he asked.

"No," she said. "I think it would be better for you if you didn't travel for a while. I think it will be best for the both of us if I made this trip alone."

"Are you going to see her about what happened last night?" he asked.

"Yes, I have to find out why I'm having this nightmare."

Two months later, John was returning to his normal routine. Sarah decided it was time to go and visit Aunt Lillian. John came into the room as she began to pack for the trip.

"How long will you be gone?" he asked.

"About three or four days. Do you think you are strong enough to manage things while I'm gone?"

"Don't worry about me," he assured her. "I'll be just fine. I'm not going to do very much anyway."

"You be careful and please, John, don't overdo it."

He assured her he would take it easy while she was away. Sarah made arrangements to take the train so she could take in some of the sights. She figured she could take a plane back. She called Aunt Lillian to let her know she was coming and when she would arrive.

Aunt Lillian was 94 years old and was able to get around with the help of a walking cane. She wanted to send one of her neighbors to meet Sarah at the train station, but Sarah told her that it wouldn't be necessary. She would take a taxi.

"Is John coming with you?" she asked.

"No, John isn't coming with me this time."

"Well, I'll have you all to myself," Aunt Lillian said with glee.

"Yes, you will," Sarah laughed.

FAMILY SECRETS

The next day, John drove Sarah to the train station. He kissed her goodbye and wished her a safe journey there and back home.

When Sarah arrived in Chicago, she got a taxi to take her to Aunt Lillian's home. Aunt Lillian was looking out the window when the taxi stopped in front of the house. As immediate as a 94-year-old woman can, she came out to greet Sarah.

"I'm so glad to see you!" she exclaimed. "You look exactly like your mother, Ruth."

Sarah smiled as she said, "You always tell me that."

Aunt Lillian smiled. "You know it's the truth," she answered. "How's John?"

"He's fine," Sarah replied. "The children were with us while he was in the hospital." As Aunt Lillan quirked her brow, Sarah began to explain the events leading up to John's heart attack.

"We almost lost the farm because of John's pride," she lamented.

"Maybe he was trying to protect you the way some men do," Aunt Lillian offered. "Some men think we're all helpless creatures wondering through life solely dependent on them to protect us from all things that aren't pleasant," Aunt Lillian said with a laugh. "I have some money put away. You could have come to me for the money, Sarah."

"I didn't know we were on the brink of losing the farm until it was almost too late to save it. John didn't tell me what was going on."

"That's just like a man," Aunt Lillian complained. "The only thing they think we're good for is cooking, cleaning, and having babies," Aunt Lillian said, her eyes twinkling. "I'm just having fun," she went on to explain. "Sarah, you have a wonderful husband and family. The Lord has really blessed you. I always wanted to marry a man like John and have a large family."

"You know, Aunt Lillian, when I was growing up, I always wanted some brothers and sisters to play with. I remember asking Santa Claus to bring me some at Christmas time. I realized, as I got older, wishing isn't the way they get here." They both laughed. "After John and I were married and I was in the delivery room with John Jr., I almost changed my mind about having a large family. Those pains made me say things I didn't know I was saying. Looking back over my life now, I wouldn't change a thing."

As the day passed, Aunt Lillian's stomach started to growl. "Sarah, are you hungry?" she asked as she rubbed her belly.

"Yes, I was just thinking about that."

"I'll fix us something to eat," she said as she rose from her chair.

"Aunt Lillian, you sit down. I'll get the food. You can be my guest while I'm here." They both laughed as Sarah started toward the kitchen. The idea that Aunt Lillian wait on her at 94 years old just didn't sit well with Sarah.

As they ate their meal, Sarah made one request. "Can we visit the cemetery tomorrow?" she asked Aunt Lillian from the kitchen.

"Yes, I would like that very much."

After breakfast the next morning, they got ready to go to the cemetery. Sarah brought the car around front for Aunt Lillian. "I see you have gotten a new set of wheels since I was here last," she remarked as she pulled the car up.

Aunt Lillian's eyes twinkled as she said, "You know I don't like anything old except dollar bills and wine. I never know when my boyfriend might be wanting to see me in a hurry."

"Aunt Lillian!" Sarah exclaimed as she cracked up laughing. 'Aunt Lillian has a wonderful sense of humor,' she thought. That was one of the reasons Sarah loved her so. It was weird because Aunt Lillian hadn't driven in years. "Do you really have a boyfriend?" Sarah asked as she wondered about Aunt Lillian's statement.

"Maybe, maybe not," she answered. "At my age, he certainly wouldn't be called a boyfriend."

On the way to the cemetery, Sarah asked Aunt Lillian why she never married after her first husband.

"I never found a man as good as John," Aunt Lillian teased her. They both smiled.

"Melissa would be about my age if she had lived, wouldn't she?" Sarah inquired about Aunt Lillian's daughter.

"Yes child, she would be about your age. I regret having her body cremated. If I hadn't, she would be here with your mother. She was the only child the Lord blessed me with, but I didn't have her for long."

When they arrived at the cemetery, they made their way to Ruth's grave. Sarah kneeled down on a towel that she had brought with her and removed the debris.

"Hi, mom. Aunt Lillian is here with me," she said as she placed a vase of long-stemmed, white roses near the head stone. "These are your favorites." Sarah turned to say something to her aunt and noticed that she was crying. She immediately got up to comfort her.

"Seeing Ruth's grave brings back a lot of memories," she explained. "Help me to the car Sarah and you can visit as long as you want." Sarah had never seen her aunt cry before. She helped her aunt up and assisted her to the car. As she returned to her mother's grave, she could still see Aunt Lillian wiping tears from her eyes. The visit had really upset her. Sarah stayed at Ruth's grave site for about 15 or 20 minutes before returning to the car.

Aunt Lillian was quiet and subdued on the way home. Sarah felt a little guilty. "I'm sorry the visit to the cemetery upset you, Aunt Lillian."

"It's not your fault. I was reminded of a lot of things I've spent my lifetime trying to forget."

"Things like what?"

"Just things, child, just things," Aunt Lillian trailed off. She lost herself in reflection as the countryside faded into yesterday.

After a while, Aunt Lillian perked up a bit. She asked Sarah to stop by the home of a new family that had recently moved into the neighborhood. "I want to welcome them to the neighborhood," she explained. "I have seen them at church, but have never been to their home. I think this is an excellent time to visit them and show you off at the same time."

Aunt Lillian smiled. She loved bragging about her family to her friends. Sarah saw her returning to her old self again. She was smiling and joking, having a good time.

Sarah pulled into the driveway of Mr. and Mrs. Mathis' home. Mrs. Mathis was working in her flower beds. She looked up as they pulled into the driveway. She thought it was her husband returning from a business meeting. She didn't recognize Sarah, but recognition lit her face when she saw Aunt Lillian.

"How are you, Lillian?" she called. "Isn't this a pleasant surprise!"

"I'm fine."

"Who is that with you, your daughter?"

"No, this is my niece, Sarah."

"Hello, pleased to meet you," Sarah replied.

"You could be Lillian's daughter. You look so much like her."

Mrs. Mathis' comment made Sarah think. She had never heard anyone say that to her before.

"Sometimes I wish she was my daughter," Aunt Lillian said. They laughed. They visited with Mrs. Mathis for a while and then went to a seafood restaurant for dinner.

"This was one of the best days of my life," Aunt Lillian sighed as they arrived home. Thank you for making this possible," she told Sarah. They stayed up a little while longer until sleep weighed their eyelids down and they were forced to turn in for the night.

During the night, the man with no face returned. Sarah could see him coming toward her as he entered the room through her door. His hands had grown. They seemed larger than in any of her dreams before. "No, no, go away," she moaned as she thrashed in her sleep. "Leave me alone!" she yelled.

Aunt Lillian was jarred awake by Sarah's screams. She called to Sarah, but Sarah didn't answer her. Sarah continued talking as if someone was in the room. Aunt Lillian thought an intruder had broken into the house and was attacking her. She grabbed her pistol and made her way to Sarah's room and turned on the light.

"You leave Sarah alone right now or I'm going to shoot!" she threatened. When her eyes focused, Aunt Lillian didn't see anyone in the room with Sarah.

"Sarah, is there someone in here with you?" she asked, bewildered. Sarah was in the bed with the covers pulled up to her face, crying.

"Sarah, what's wrong? Are you all right?"

"I've been having this same nightmare for quite a while now. I'm sorry to disturb you with this," Sarah responded shakily.

"When did it start?" Aunt Lillian asked as she sat down on the edge of Sarah's bed. She placed her hand on Sarah's shoulder as she waited for her answer. "Melissa, this nightmare has got to let you go. It has bothered you long enough," she said, shaking her head.

"Aunt Lillian?"

"Yes dear?"

"You called me Melissa."

"I did?"

"Yes, you did."

"I'm sorry. I don't know why that came out. I guess I'm getting old. I'm not as good with names as I used to be."

Sarah looked over at the pistol. "I didn't know you had a pistol, Aunt Lillian."

"Child, you need some type of protection these days."

"Do you know how to use it?"

"I think I do. If someone was in here bothering you, I guess we both would have found out tonight," Aunt Lillian said with a laugh. She got up to leave the room. "Are you going to be all right?" she asked as she headed to bed.

"Yes, I'll be all right. Please leave the light on, though."

"Okay," Aunt Lillian said quietly as she shuffled out of the door.

The next morning, Sarah made breakfast and was having a cup of coffee when Aunt Lillian woke up. She called to Sarah and asked if she was okay.

"Yes, I'm having a cup of coffee. Would you like some?"

"Let me get these old bones moving and I'll be right there," she said.

A few minutes later, Aunt Lillian made her way to the kitchen. Sarah was looking out the window sipping on a cup of coffee. Sarah poured Aunt Lillian a cup and sat it on the table.

"Thank you," Aunt Lillian said.

"Aunt Lillian, do you remember calling me Melissa last night?"

"Yes," Aunt Lillian said as she looked up at Sarah. "I guess I got confused. I was very concerned about you last night. Tell me about the nightmare. Maybe if you talk about it, it will go away."

"It started when I was very young. Did I ever mention it?" she asked.

"No, I don't recall you ever mentioning it to me."

"Well, anyway, I used to wake up talking and screaming. The man never has a face! I just want him to leave me alone. I never could see his face, only these hands coming toward me. I hadn't had one in years. It started again the night John came home from the hospital. I don't know if the trauma of John's heart attack triggered something inside me. The nightmare is just as frightening now as it was when I was a child. I feel there is something in my past that's causing me to have this nightmare." Sarah sat her cup of coffee down and leveled her eyes on Aunt Lillian. "Do you know of anything that happened in my past that could have started this thing?"

Aunt Lillian paused for a moment. "You sure do make a wonderful cup of coffee" she told Sarah. Sarah knew that Aunt Lillian was hiding something because she hadn't answered the question.

"Aunt Lillian, you know the reason why, don't you? I have no one else I can turn to. If you know, you have to tell me. I can't continue through life screaming in the middle of the night."

Aunt Lillian didn't say a word. She got up from the table and went into her bedroom, closing the door behind her. She stayed in her room for about three hours. She had seen the determined look on Sarah's face and it worried her.

Baffled, but determined, Sarah wondered what had come over Aunt Lillian. When she finally came out of her room and sat down, Sarah asked her again. "If you know anything, even if it hurts me, please tell me the truth. I really need to know what happened."

"I was hoping I would never have this conversation with you. Sometimes things are better if they are left as they are. Old memories can reopen deep wounds. I had a feeling when you called and said that you were coming alone on this trip that it wouldn't be like the rest. The answer to your question is yes," Aunt Lillian sighed. "I know what happened to you that brought about this nightmare."

"Before you were born," Aunt Lillian continued, "your mother was a beautiful woman. That is what she was told by most of the people she knew at the time. She was a strong-willed woman, determined to succeed in life. She worked during the day and went to college at night. When your mother met your father, they fell in love, but I believe he was intimidated by her beauty and success. He never mentioned it, but I believe it was true. Your parents were not married when you were born."

Sarah looked at Aunt Lillian in amazement as she went on. "Your mother got pregnant by your father, out of wedlock. When you were about one year old, a man broke into the house while you were home alone with your mother. She could not defend you and herself against the man. He threatened to harm you if she didn't let him have his way with her. You heard and saw everything that happened that night. After witnessing what happened, you were afraid to sleep alone. You kept asking if the man with no face was coming back. That is how you referred to him even then. He wore a black ski mask over his face. His hands were the only things you could see and identify. That is how your nightmare began. After I told your father, he asked me not to go to the police. He said if I did that, my reputation would be ruined. He told me that he and I should get married right away. We were married two months later."

"What do you mean, you told my father?" Sarah interrupted.

"Sarah, I know this is going to be a shock to you, but please try to understand and forgive me. Your first name was Melissa. I'm your mother, not Ruth."

This information hit Sarah like a ton of bricks falling on top of her head. Sarah was speechless. She stared at Aunt Lillian, her mouth hanging wide open as Aunt Lillian finished her story.

"After I married your father, Ruth would take you home with her for the weekend. You two got along so well and you didn't have the nightmares as often when you were with her. Eventually, they stopped all together. Your father, Ruth, and I agreed that you should stay with her for a while. Days turned into weeks, weeks into months, and before we realized it, a year had passed. You started calling Ruth mommy and she started calling you Sarah. Six months later, we had your name legally changed to Sarah. That is why Melissa isn't buried next to Ruth out there. You are Melissa. I created the story about her being cremated so you wouldn't ask where she was buried. We thought we were giving you a new start in life, one without nightmares. Your father stayed with me about eight months after your name was changed and then he left. Our relationship was never the same after I was raped. I believe the reason he didn't want me to go to the police was because of what people would say about him more so than his concern for me. I never wanted to have this conversation with you. I thought everything was working out just fine. I wanted to take these secrets to the grave with me. If the nightmare hadn't returned, you never would have known."

Sarah was astonished at what she was hearing. "Are you saying that you're my mother instead of mama?" she croaked out woodenly.

"That's exactly what I'm saying. Your name was legally changed from Melissa to Sarah. I have your birth certificate and the legal document changing your name from Melissa to Sarah.

The truth was more than Sarah had bargained for. "I'm so confused," she said as tears rolled down her face.

"I know this is confusing and it hurts," Aunt Lillian told her, "but you said you wanted to know the truth."

"My name is Melissa and it was changed to Sarah."

"That's right."

"You're my birth mother, not my aunt?"

"Yes, I'm your mother."

Without saying another word, Sarah went to her room and closed the door. Aunt Lillian didn't know how Sarah was going to react to all of this. She felt as if a heavy load had been lifted from her shoulders. The truth was finally out. However emotionally Sarah reacted, she would have to accept it. When she emerged from her room, she could love Aunt Lillian or hate her for keeping this secret for all these years. Thinking about the outcome was more than she could handle at the moment.

Aunt Lillian felt naked sitting there waiting for Sarah to come out and announce her verdict of love and compassion or hatred and condemnation. She knew she had exposed her life to Sarah, not knowing what she would think. 'I'm praying for forgiveness and understanding,' she thought to herself.

Aunt Lillian had been quite successful in her life. She had overcome the tragedy of rape without therapy or professional help. She was well-respected in her town and community. People often sought her out for advice on business and personal matters. Despite her social standing, she wasn't feeling very good about herself at present.

When Sarah came out of her room, she still couldn't help wondering if Aunt Lillian had told her the truth. Before she could say anything, Aunt Lillian handed her the birth papers and told her to read them for herself.

"John and I are just alike," Aunt Lillian said. "We both tried to shelter you from the hurt and pain. We both did a miserable job at it and we both acted out of love for you and nothing else. I'm an old woman who has learned a lot over the years. There are some things I wish I had handled differently. This is one of them. I wish I had told you when you were old enough to understand. You and Ruth had developed a close relationship and I didn't want to bring back those awful memories of that awful night."

"Aunt Lillian, who was my father?"

"Ruth and I always told you the truth about your father. You were told he died when you were three years old and that's the truth."

"Did you ever find out who raped you?"

"Yes, I knew who he was the night it happened. I was afraid to call his name because he might have killed us both."

"I have kept up with his career and place of residence over the years," Aunt Lillian told her in a flat voice. "He has been married three times. He is presently with his third wife and I understand that this marriage is on the rocks also. He has had a very successful career, but he has never had a successful marriage. Judge Ray Barnes," she said monotonously, "the celebrated civil rights attorney and judge."

"Are you telling me that Judge Ray Barnes is the man who raped you?" Sarah asked incredulously, staring at Aunt Lillian's blank face.

"Yes, he is the man. At the time, he had not attended law school. He had tried to date me several times, but I wasn't interested in him. The Honorable Judge Ray Barnes is the one who traumatized our lives. About three months after I was raped, I got a .45 pistol and waited outside his home to kill him. I was dressed in black and wore a ski mask, just as he had. When he drove into the driveway and parked, I confronted him with the pistol. I motioned for him to get out of the car and get down on his knees. I tried to pull the trigger, but something stopped me. He begged for his life. He offered me all of his money and possessions. I never said a word. After seeing him beg for his life, I backed away and ran down the street. I just couldn't do it. I never saw him again except on the television or in the newspaper. That night, I regained my self-respect, although the hurt never went away. When you're raped, you lose something very precious. It is hard to regain. Your body is violated in the worst way because you didn't give your consent for it to happen."

"Aunt Lillian, why didn't you pull the trigger?" Sarah asked. Had it been her, she didn't think the judge would have been so lucky.

"I think the reason I didn't was because the Lord showed me how small a man really is when he is begging on his knees for his life. I held his life in my hands for a few minutes and I chose to let him keep it. That was the satisfaction I needed so that I could get on with my healing."

"Aunt Lillian, you're quite a woman," Sarah reflected. "It must have taken real restraint not to pull that trigger."

"I'm glad you think so," Aunt Lillian responded, thinking how empty she'd have felt afterwards.

As fate would have it, the next morning Sarah and Aunt Lillian decided to go out for breakfast. As they left the breakfast bar at the restaurant, Aunt Lillian saw Judge Ray Barnes walk through the door. She didn't say anything to Sarah, she just sat down and started to eat her breakfast.

Sarah was very talkative. She was enjoying her Aunt Lillian's company and trying on the possibility of getting to know her as a mother, when it dawned on her that Aunt Lillian was angry. She hadn't spoken much since they sat down and she had a frown fixed on her face.

"What's wrong?" Sarah asked her. There was no immediate answer. "Is it something I said?" Sarah plied on. Still Aunt Lillian didn't answer. "Do you want to go home?" Sarah tried.

"No," she finally replied. "I want to finish my breakfast."

"Please, tell me what's wrong," Sarah said as she looked at Aunt Lillian. She was really starting to get worried.

"Look over my left shoulder at the gentleman seated at the table in the corner." Sarah looked and saw four men seated at a table talking and laughing.

"There are four men seated there. Which one are you referring to?"

Aunt Lillian turned. "The one with the glasses and the bald head," she said.

"Yes, I see him. He looks very distinguished. Who is he?"

Aunt Lillian paused for a moment. "That's the devil we were talking about last night. That's Judge Ray Barnes." Sarah's fork slipped from her fingers and clattered to her plate. She looked in the direction of his table. All of a sudden, they both lost their appetites.

Judge Ray Barnes noticed them looking in his direction. The smile on his face slowly slid away as he realized who Aunt Lillian was. His friends continued to talk, but he didn't say another word. He began shifting his food around in his plate as he occasionally stole glances in their direction.

Sarah noticed that he had become uncomfortable. "Does he know who we are?" Sarah asked Aunt Lillian. Aunt Lillian busied herself with gathering her belongings and told Sarah she was ready to go.

"Okay," Sarah said as she quickly finished her orange juice. Judge Barnes and his party left before they had a chance to exit the restaurant. Aunt Lillian and Sarah stayed seated long enough for them to leave.

As Sarah was driving home on the freeway, she noticed the traffic had stopped. The cars behind her stopped as she slowed down. Some of the passengers had left their cars and walked down the freeway to see what had happened. She heard someone say that there had been a terrible accident and a man had been killed. The traffic decreased to a crawl and they began to slowly move down the freeway. As Sarah passed the accident, Aunt Lillian commented about the vehicles involved. One was a passenger car and the other was a tractor-trailer rig. She recognized one of the accident victims as one of the men sitting with Judge Barnes in the restaurant.

"Wasn't that one of the men with Judge Barnes at the restaurant?" Sarah questioned.

"I believe it was, Sarah."

Neither commented on the body on the gurney being placed into the ambulance while another man was being attended by paramedics. They were both quiet until they pulled into the driveway.

"Do you think the man on the gurney was Judge Barnes?" Sarah asked.

"If it was him, I hope he's dead. I hope he goes straight to hell," Aunt Lillian replied venomously. Sarah understood why she was feeling the way she was. Aunt Lillian was carrying around a lot of bitterness from long ago.

Before going to bed, Sarah called John to see how he was doing. He sounded groggy as he answered the phone.

"Hi, honey, it's Sarah."

"Hi, princess," he sleepily replied. "How are you doing?"

"I'm fine. Is everything okay?"

"It would be better if you were here."

"John, I have so much to tell you about my trip."

"How is Aunt Lillian?"

"She's fine. She's still getting around on her cane," Sarah explained. "She bought a new car."

"Is she driving again?" he asked.

"No, she isn't driving. I believe those days are over. The mystery is who is driving her when I'm not here. I've been doing all the driving since my arrival."

"Are you coming back by train or plane?"

"I'll probably make my reservation tomorrow. I think I'll come back by plane."

"Well, call me on Saturday and let me know where to meet you so I can be there when you arrive."

"I love you and miss you so."

"I love you too, John. I'm looking forward to getting home. Goodnight."

"Goodnight my love."

The next morning, about 6 a.m., the doorbell rang. The sound woke Sarah and Aunt Lillian from their sleep.

"Who is it?" Sarah asked from behind the door. By the time Aunt Lillian reached the front door, Sarah was engrossed in a conversation with a man. They were talking about an accident.

"Who had an accident?" Aunt Lillian asked as she came in on the outskirts of the conversation. Sarah and the man looked at Aunt Lillian, but neither of them said a word.

"Who had an accident?" Aunt Lillian repeated. "Are you going to tell me who was involved in the accident you were talking about?"

"Aunt Lillian, please sit down."

"Who is this man?" Aunt Lillian asked as she complied with Sarah's request.

"My name is Charles Carter," he said as he stepped forward. "I'm sorry to wake you up so early this morning, but I was sent to give you a message."

"About what and from whom?" she asked.

"I'm Judge Barnes' assistant."

"I don't want to hear anymore. Sir, please leave my house," she said as she rose from her chair. She started to walk away when she heard Sarah call to her.

"Aunt Lillian, please, just hear him out."

"What's the message?" Aunt Lillian grated out, her back turned to them.

"He asks that you come and see him."

Aunt Lillian was furious! "Why would I want to see this man?!" she exclaimed. "He has caused me enough pain in my life!"

"He's dying, Miss Lillian. He was involved in a very serious accident yesterday. The doctors don't expect him to last very long."

"I have nothing to say to him," Aunt Lillian countered. "I don't ever want to see his face again." She turned and walked to her bedroom, closing the door behind her.

"I'm sorry for the inconvenience," Mr. Carter told Sarah as he left the house.

Sarah made coffee and asked if Aunt Lillian wanted a cup.

"Yes, come on in."

When Sarah entered the room, Aunt Lillian was wiping tears from her face.

"You really do make good coffee," she said after tasting the brew. "Sarah. What do you think I should do?"

"Aunt Lillian, I don't know. You have very strong emotions eating away at you because of what happened that dreadful night. Maybe this is the beginning of a new healing process. We need to put this behind us once and for all."

Aunt Lillian thought about it for a while. She made a decision to visit Judge Barnes in the hospital.

"Okay, find out which hospital and where it is," Aunt Lillian said as she got up to get dressed. She was waiting at the door as Sarah pulled the car around. On their way to the hospital, Aunt Lillian prayed that she would have strength enough for her confrontation with her rapist.

When they arrived at the hospital, Sarah stopped the car at the main entrance to let Aunt Lillian out. She parked the car and joined Aunt Lillian who was sitting on a bench watching a flock of birds in a nearby tree.

"They are so beautiful," she sighed as Sarah joined her. They took a moment and got up to go into the hospital. They made their way through to the elevator. They were silent as the elevator lifted them toward their destination. They got off the elevator, walked down the hall, and found Judge Barnes' room.

As they approached his room, they saw a gathering of people near the end of the hall. One of them was the man who had come to see them that morning, Mr. Carter. He had a sad look on his face as he met them.

"I'm glad you decided to come to see him, but unfortunately, it's too late. He died 20 minutes ago." After imparting the news, he asked them to wait a moment while he located someone who would like to see them. He went into the room and returned a couple of minutes later with a lady.

"This is Margaret, Judge Barnes' wife," he said.

"You're Lillian, aren't you?" the lady asked as she looked at Aunt Lillian.

"Yes," Aunt Lillian answered. "This is my niece," Aunt Lillian replied.

"I'm pleased to meet you both," Margaret offered as she smiled at them. "I wish our meeting was under different circumstances. Ray was hoping you would come before he passed away. He had something important that he wanted to tell you. He kept it to himself. He wouldn't even tell me. He called your name several times before he passed."

Aunt Lillian felt like Judge Barnes had abused her all over again. 'The old bastard died just before we arrived as if to say he's still one up on me' she thought. 'I shouldn't have come anyway.'

Sarah was concerned about Aunt Lillian. She was hoping Judge Barnes would have apologized before he died. 'It would mean a lot to my aunt to hear him say it,' she thought.

"I need to lie down," Aunt Lillian said when they got home.

"Are you hungry?" Sarah asked her.

"No," Aunt Lillian replied as she headed toward her room.

'Lord, please help her through this,' Sarah prayed as she watched Aunt Lillian leave the room.

It was late afternoon by the time Aunt Lillian came back out. She ate and went back to bed. Sarah looked in on her just before retiring for the night. Aunt Lillian was resting comfortably with her Bible in her hand.

At breakfast the next morning, Aunt Lillian apologized to Sarah for sleeping the afternoon away.

"Did you sleep well?" Sarah asked her.

"Pretty good, under the circumstances."

As they were finishing their breakfast, the doorbell rang.

"I wonder who that could be," Aunt Lillian said. "I'll get it." She waved Sarah back to her seat.

"I can get it for you," Sarah offered.

"No, child, I'll get it. This is something I do all the time when you aren't here," she said, smiling as she walked to the door. She looked through the peephole. "Who is it?" she called.

"I'm with UPS and I have a package for Miss Lillian," a young man called from the other side of the door. Aunt Lillian opened the door and signed for the package.

"Thank you," she said. "Have a nice day," she told him as she accepted the package.

"Who's it from?" Sarah asked as she entered the room.

"I don't know," she replied as she walked over to a chair and sat down. Inside the package, she found a letter with no return address. When Aunt Lillian opened the letter, she could see the words **"I'M SO SORRY FOR WHAT I DID TO YOU AND YOUR DAUGHTER. I WAS A FOOLISH YOUNG MAN, TOO CAUGHT UP IN THE WAYS OF THE WORLD. PLEASE FORGIVE ME."**

Aunt Lillian froze in shock. Shaking and crying, she let the letter slip from her hands and float to the floor.

"What's wrong?" Sarah asked her, worried about Aunt Lillian's response to the package. She went over to where Aunt Lillian was sitting and picked up the letter from the floor. When she saw the first page, she knew it was from Judge Barnes. Sarah knelt on the floor in front of Aunt Lillian's chair.

"Aunt Lillian," she said, "it's going to be all right. Everything is going to be all right." She reached out and took Aunt Lillian's hands.

"You need to read the rest of the letter," she encouraged.

"I can't read it."

"Then I'll read it if you think you can listen to it's content," Sarah offered.

"I'll listen if you'll read," Aunt Lillian acquiesced. Sarah opened the letter and began to read. The letter was dated ten days earlier.

∾

Lillian, I don't know if you will ever read this letter. I'm compelled by conscience and my actions long ago to try to show my regret and remorse for the crime I committed against you. It was a horrible thing to do. That night has haunted me all of my life, as it must have haunted you and your daughter. You were such a beautiful woman and I had this fantasy of having sex with you. It occupied my mind day and night. I used to watch you walking about. You were so full of life. I could see the expressions of joy and happiness on the faces of the people that were with you. I was almost afraid to talk to you because my self-esteem was so low. When I did get up enough nerve to ask you out, you said no. I was crushed so badly that it made me more determined than ever to be with you. I became insanely foolish. I couldn't stand to be rejected by you.

I realized later, as I should have then, it was your prerogative to be with whomever you wanted to. I had no right forcing myself on you. I realize I altered the course of your life and other people around you, especially your daughter. After leaving your home that night, I was afraid to go home. I thought every police car I saw was coming for me. I stayed with a friend for three days. For about three months, I had nightmares about the police coming to arrest me. I would wake up, in a panic, soaking wet with perspiration. The guilt I was carrying almost drove me crazy. I had a feeling you might have known who I was. You asked me not to hurt your daughter and almost called my name. I pretended not to hear you.

Oh, Lillian, I wish I could undue all of this. I'm a criminal that has never been brought to justice. I have never paid for the terrible crime I committed. Again, I'm sorry. I should never have done this terrible thing. At the time, I couldn't help myself. Being a judge, I know there is no excuse for what I did. The night you approached me in the driveway, I knew it was you. I thought I was going to die that night. I guess I felt a little of what you and your daughter felt. I have woken up many nights hearing the frantic cry of a baby. When it first started, about ten years ago, I didn't realize it was the cry of your daughter until months later when I saw her face in one of my dreams.

I assume you're wondering why I became a lawyer. I never aspired to be a lawyer until after that night. The irony of it all is that I was a criminal, a fugitive from justice who decided to become a lawyer and try to help people. After you didn't come forward, I thought you may have forgiven me and I had a new opportunity to do something with my life. I had never considered going to law school before this happened. I didn't think I was intelligent enough.

When I graduated from law school, I took the bar exam three times before passing. The very first case I tried was a rape case, similar to my own. I tried not to take it, but for some reason, it was destined for me. I won the case for this young lady. For the first time in my life, I felt a sense of accomplishment. I was in a profession where I could make a difference. I have represented many rape victims during my career. Everyone has reminded me of you.

I have been married three times. The first two ended in divorce. The woman I'm married to now is very understanding. Although we've had our problems, we're still together. I still go through states of depression. She asked me to see a psychiatrist to find out what's wrong. I haven't told her that I know what's causing it. Sometimes I want to tell her, but I'm afraid of what she might think of me afterward. I've felt like a prisoner all of my life. Maybe all of us involved have been prisoners. I've never had children of my own. My first two wives had miscarriages. My current wife didn't want children, but I've always wanted children. I guess that's part of my punishment.

My life has been filled with a lot of success for the people I have represented over the years, but for me, I have felt like a failure ever since I left your house that night. I have had brief moments of jubilation after winning cases, but after the crowd is gone, I'm always reminded of that night. I have passed out sentences from probation to death, but every time I sentence a rapist, it is as if I'm sentencing myself.

Over the years, it has taken a heavy toll on me. I travel in a circle of high profile people, but I'm the loneliest man in town. As a judge, I have sat in judgment on countless cases. In analyzing mine, it seems to me that I was sentenced by fate a long time ago. All I can do is once again say I'm sorry for my actions.

Respectfully Yours,

Judge Ray Barnes

SARAH MEETS BEN

"The old bastard had a heart after all!" Aunt Lillian thought. "He was wrong about not having a child. He does have one."

"Aunt Lillian, what do you mean?" Sarah asked. "How do you know about this child?"

"Sarah, I got pregnant the night I was raped. Ruth is the only one in the family who knew about it. That is the reason why you went to stay with Ruth so long."

"Aunt Lillian, do you mean that I have a brother or sister out there somewhere?"

"Yes, that's exactly what I mean. You have a brother."

"Where is he? Did you give him up for adoption?"

"Yes."

"He could be anywhere! Do you know if he's okay? Is he well?"

"Slow down, Sarah. The answer to all of your questions is yes." Tears slid down Aunt Lillian's face as the memories flooded back. "Lord, what have I done?" she asked. "Sarah, I couldn't keep him. I just couldn't handle it. I know the child had nothing to do with what happened to us, but I just couldn't handle looking at him. I was devastated after being raped. About a month later, I found out I was pregnant. I asked Ruth to keep you so I could deal with my pregnancy. I thought about having an abortion, but I was strong enough to decide against that. Just before I started showing, I went away until I had the baby. I met the couple that adopted him before he was born. They were having problems having children of their own so they were looking for a young child to adopt. They adopted Ben and gave him a fine home. Oh, that's his name, Benjamin Davis."

"Do you know where they live, Aunt Lillian?"

"Yes, I do," Aunt Lillian told her. "He lives in Detroit, Michigan. His adopted parents and I had an agreement before he was born. It allowed me to maintain contact with him as a friend of the family. I used to visit him once a year when he was growing up. When I wanted to give him things I would send them to Mr. and Mrs. Davis and they would give them to him. They are both doctors. They provided Ben with a loving home and a good education. Ben is a doctor also. He works for the Center for Disease Control in Atlanta, GA. He's the doctor in charge of a study searching for ways to prevent and hopefully to find a cure for the AIDS virus. So you see, Sarah, his life has turned out rather well."

"Are you going to tell Ben about the rest of his family? Are you going to tell him who his real father is? Are you going to tell him who his biological father is before he is lowered into the ground?"

"Not so fast, Sarah," Aunt Lillian warned. "I don't have the right to interfere in their lives. That is part of our agreement. I promised not to acknowledge myself as Ben's mother under any circumstances."

"Aunt Lillian, he's your flesh and blood!" Sarah said. "And he's my only brother. I realize the importance of keeping promises, but these are very unusual circumstances. For years, I thought that I was an only child. Now, I'm told I have a brother. I thought you were my aunt and you told me that you're my mother. I don't fully understand why things are happening so fast, but we can't stop now. We must at least try to set things straight. Ben must be told about you and his father. I don't want to destroy his life, but I would like to have an opportunity to be a part of his life and he a part of ours. Are there any more secrets that you haven't revealed to me?"

"No, child," Aunt Lillian responded tiredly. "There aren't any more secrets. Sarah, I don't know about approaching the Davis' about this situation."

"How much do you know about Ben personally, Aunt Lillian?"

"I know he's married. He and his wife have a stable marriage and two wonderful children."

"So, you're a grandmother," Sarah added.

"Yes, I am," Aunt Lillian answered. "They have a boy, Christopher, and a girl, Catrina."

"I have a niece and a nephew," Sarah said. She was so excited. "Aunt Lillian, don't you believe it's worth a try to unite our family?"

"Sarah, this is happening so fast. Maybe you shouldn't have come here. We can't go around destroying people's lives. Mr. and Mrs. Davis are up in years, like me. Suppose this causes them physical harm? I don't want that on my conscience."

"Aunt Lillian, I sympathize with you concerning their health and well-being, but the knowledge you have concealed all these years is important in setting our family free. The hand that was dealt us was unfortunate indeed, but it's the only hand we have. There are reasons why things are happening the way they are. I certainly don't understand the urgency of it all, but I feel in my heart that it's all a part of destiny. We aren't bad people, Aunt Lillian. We pose no threat of harm to anyone. I think we need to see this through. I have said what I feel in my heart. The final decision is yours. If you decide not to pursue it any further, I will abide by your decision."

"Sarah, I'll pray about it," Aunt Lillian reluctantly sighed. "I'll give you my decision in the morning." This trip was proving to be extremely tiring for Aunt Lillian. Too many things were happening at once. She'd have to think long and hard about how to proceed.

It was a long night for Sarah. The uncertainty of Aunt Lillian's decision made her restless. She didn't sleep well. When she woke up the next morning, she made breakfast and waited for Aunt Lillian. She finally emerged from her room around noon. She told Sarah that she would call the Davis' and see if they could go and see them. "I'll make airline reservations, I know this is very difficult for you. I've always known you as a woman of integrity and for you to even consider doing this compromises your principles. I truly believe we're all going to be blessed in ways we don't understand. I love you Aunt Lillian."

After boarding the plane to Detroit, Sarah and Aunt Lillian were extremely quiet. There were so many things going through their minds. This was going to be a very long day indeed.

Upon their arrival at the airport, Mr. Davis was there to greet them. They exchanged greetings and then got on their way to his home.

"You didn't tell us you were bringing such a lovely companion with you, Lillian," he said, looking at Sarah.

"I'm sorry I forgot to mention it last night when we spoke. I hope it won't be an inconvenience for you."

"Of course not. We're glad to have the company."

"I'm sorry, Mr. Davis, this is my daughter, Sarah. Sarah, this is Mr. Frank Davis."

"You never mentioned you had a daughter, Lillian," Mr. Davis said, surprised as he shook Sarah's hand.

"Mr. Davis," Sarah told him, "I'm glad to meet you."

"The pleasure is all mine, Sarah. Just call me Frank. Most people do."

When they arrived, Mr. Davis' wife, Patricia, greeted them at the door. Mr. Davis introduced Sarah to his wife and told her that she was Lillian's daughter.

"I didn't know you had a daughter, Lillian," Patricia replied.

"I don't believe I have mentioned her before," Aunt Lillian told her. "Sarah is my only daughter."

"Well, come in and relax," Patricia offered. "Would you like to go to a bedroom to get comfortable?"

"I would like to change my shoes, if you don't mind," Aunt Lillian told her.

"Come this way, I'll show you to your room," Mrs. Davis told them as she shuffled down the hall. She had detected an urgency in Lillian's voice last night.

"Is there something going on?" Patricia asked them, suspiciously.

"Well, there's something I need to talk to you about," Lillian nervously replied.

"It's about Ben, isn't it?"

"Yes, Patricia, it is."

Mrs. Davis told Aunt Lillian to get comfortable and when she was ready, they would have a bite to eat. Then, they could talk. Frank had overheard the conversation and asked if there was something wrong with Ben. Mrs. Davis assured him that Ben was fine.

"He's supposed to be here tomorrow to attend a conference on the AIDS virus. Come on, Frank, let them change into something comfortable. We can talk later."

It took about five minutes for Aunt Lillian and Sarah to change. When they returned from their rooms, Mr. and Mrs. Davis were discussing something on the couch. They stopped when they saw their guests.

"Would you like something to eat?" Mrs. Davis asked. "Maybe some coffee, orange juice, or milk?"

"Coffee," they said in unison.

"I was going to fix some bacon, eggs, and toast. Will that be okay with you?" Patricia asked.

"That will be just fine," they told her.

"Lillian, why are you here?" Mr. Davis asked. "I know you didn't come to Detroit just to pay us a social visit. I know there is something on your mind so let's have it."

"Frank, don't jump to conclusions. Wait until Lillian tells us why she and Sarah are here. Lillian, why didn't you tell us you had a daughter?" Mrs. Davis questioned.

"Frank, Patricia, my intentions are not to hurt you. We're not here to destroy your relationship with Ben. You will never lose him. You are the only parents he has ever known. I never told you the reason I gave Ben up for adoption," she told them. As she looked in their eyes, she hesitated. Gathering her courage, she continued with what she had to say, "I was raped and became pregnant. The night the rape happened, Sarah was there with me. She was a little girl, about a year old. She saw the whole thing."

"What a terrible thing for you and your daughter to experience," Frank gasped. "Did you report it to the police? Did they find the guy who raped you?"

"No, I never did report it to the police, but I know who raped me."

"Does this rape have anything to do with Ben?" he continued.

"Yes, it does. I got pregnant with Ben that night," Aunt Lillian answered.

"How did all of this affect Sarah?" he asked, looking over at Sarah.

"At the time, her name was Melissa. She began having nightmares that have just recently recurred. My sister, Ruth, took her in. We had noticed that she didn't have the nightmares when she was at Ruth's home. Ruth started calling her Sarah and I eventually changed her name to Sarah. I wanted her to have a life free of the nightmares. I loved her enough to give her that. While Sarah was living with Ruth, I gave birth to Ben. I had to leave my home during my last months of pregnancy so people wouldn't notice."

"Lillian, we're deeply sorry about all of your problems, but we had an agreement that you are supposed to honor. After all these years, why are you here with your daughter? Are you trying to ruin our lives?" Mrs. Davis asked bitterly.

Aunt Lillian didn't like her tone. "Patricia," Aunt Lillian said, "I'm a woman of integrity. I made an agreement with you concerning Ben and I will honor it. Those nightmares of Sarah's recurred about 2 months ago. She came to me for answers and, during our conversations, I revealed to her that I am her mother."

"Who is the bastard that raped you, Lillian?" Mr. Davis asked again, attempting to redirect the conversation before they exploded on one another. The room was pulsing with tension.

"His name is Ray Barnes or it was anyway. He died a couple of days ago."

"You mean Judge Ray Barnes?" Mr. Davis clarified, incredulously.

"Yes, he's the one, Frank. You'll always be Ben's father. I'm not here to destroy your relationship with Ben. Judge Ray Barnes was in a terrible accident a few days ago. The day of the accident, we saw him in a restaurant where he was having lunch. He and his party left before we did and they were involved in a car accident that eventually took his life. Early the next morning, one of Judge Barnes' aids came to our home to inform us of what happened. Judge Barnes requested to see me. It took some time for me to decide to go and I wouldn't have gone without Sarah's encouragement. By the time we arrived, he had passed on. The next morning, I received an overnight package with this letter inside."

Aunt Lillian withdrew the letter from her purse and handed it to Mrs. Davis. She asked them to read it. She listened intently as Mrs. Davis removed the letter from its envelope and began to read aloud. When she finished, Aunt Lillian continued her explanation.

"The contents of this letter and the culmination of events which have occurred recently are what brought me to see you. I believe it is time to set the record straight and tell the truth. I'm not here to do anything against your wishes. The agreement we have, as I have said, I will honor. You are the only parents Ben has ever known. You have done the things parents are supposed to do. Nothing and no one can change that."

Sarah had been quiet until now, letting her mother explain the circumstances that had led them to this place in time. Now, she felt compelled to express her opinions.

"Mr. and Mrs. Davis," she began, "a short time ago, I learned of a chain of events that I had to adjust to rather quickly. In the process, I have gained another mother. I can't say that I'm over the shock, but I'm learning to deal with it, day by day. I have learned the origin of those terrifying nightmares that have plagued me all of my life. Although we have just met, I realize you have been major participants in our lives. You're part of our extended family. I grew up believing that I was the only child. Now, I have a brother whom I have never seen. I want the opportunity to get to know him and his family. Aunt Lillian and I are not here to destroy your relationships with Ben, we're here to try to enhance all of our relationships through a deeper understanding that will require each of us to grow to a higher plane. We must bring this to a conclusion soon so that you can decide if you want to tell Ben about Judge Barnes. He'll be buried the day after tomorrow. I think," she continued, "he should decide for himself if he wants to attend."

"I don't believe we have the right to tell Ben anything," Aunt Lillian interjected.

"What about me, Aunt Lillian?" Sarah asked. "What about my family? We are all a part of this family tree."

"You're right," Aunt Lillian replied.

Sarah was getting nervous. She felt so close to Ben, but she could see him slipping away. "It's not our decision to make," Aunt Lillian emphatically added. She could see the hurt in Sarah's eyes, but she knew that if Ben were to be told, it had to come from his parents. She looked at the Davis' as she spoke her next words.

"These are the circumstances under which we came to your home. We came to convey this information to you. If you think it's important enough for Ben to know, you can inform him. You're his parents." After she finished speaking, they were all quiet. She had appealed to their conscience to do the right thing. Nothing was in her hands at this time.

A few minutes later, there was a knock at the front door. The knock surprised everyone. Mr. Davis rose to answer the front door. Before he could reach it, he heard a key turn in the lock and the door slowly opened.

"Hi, Ben," Mr. Davis croaked as he watched his son walk into the house. "What a surprise."

"Hi, dad. I thought I would come over early and surprise you," Ben said with a smile.

"You most certainly did surprise us," Mrs. Davis said as she hurried over to his side and hugged him fiercely, almost possessively. "How is the family?" she asked.

"They're doing just fine. Great, actually," Ben responded as he looked around the room. He felt as if he had interrupted something. "Beverly sends her love. She is going to try to come with me on my next conference. Christopher, Catrina and the grandchildren told me to give you both their love. We all had dinner together last weekend"

"Oh! Where are my manners?" Mrs. Davis exclaimed as she realized she had not introduced Lillian and Sarah. "There are some people I want you to meet."

Sarah and Aunt Lillian had both overheard the conversation. They knew it was Ben. Sarah was both excited and afraid. She was excited to see and meet her brother, but she was afraid her emotions would get the best of her and she wouldn't be able to control herself. Aunt Lillian and Sarah looked at each other, not knowing what to expect.

"Let me take off my coat," Ben said. "I'll be right there."

When Ben came into the room, Mrs. Davis rose and introduced him to their guests. "Ben, I want you to meet Ms. Lillian and her daughter, Sarah." Sarah wanted to add to Mrs. Davis' statement and tell Ben that she was his sister and Ms. Lillian was his mother, but she held her tongue. She choked back her emotions and tried very hard not to show her true feelings.

"Ben, I am so pleased to make your acquaintance," Sarah said. "I'm pleased to have the opportunity to finally meet you. I've heard a great deal about you and your work." In response, Ben looked at Sarah and smiled.

"It's good to see you again, Ben," Aunt Lillian said. Ben gave her a puzzled look. "Have we met before?" he asked.

"I used to visit your parents when you were a young boy. You're quite a man, I hear. Your parents have told us that you are currently working on a way to prevent the AIDS virus and hopefully find a cure."

"I see they have told you quite a lot," Ben answered, grinning. "The work is very important and we have made progress, but we have a long way to go. I do believe the cure will be found. The question everyone is asking is how long will it take? The answer, unfortunately, is that no one knows. The research to bring this monster under control continues all over the world. I'm afraid many lives will be lost before the cure is found," he said. "Are either of you in the medical profession?" he asked.

Aunt Lillian shook her head no as Sarah stated, "I'm just a concerned housewife."

"That's where the prevention of AIDS must start, in the home, by being informed with the truth about the virus and teaching your family," Ben told her.

Sarah was very impressed with Ben. 'I wish I could explain everything in a way that would make everyone understand. Then, we could become one happy family,' she thought to herself.

It was about lunchtime. Mrs. Davis excused herself to make lunch for everyone. Sarah followed her into the kitchen, offering to help.

"Mrs. Davis…." she started.

"Call me Pat."

"Okay, Mrs. Davis, I mean Pat."

"Sarah, how large is your family?" Patricia interrupted.

"Well, I have a wonderful husband, John. We have five boys and three girls."

"You certainly have a large family," Patricia replied.

"When I was growing up, I was a very lonely child," Sarah explained. "I didn't have anyone to play with. I decided that when I got married, I was going to have a large family. After the first baby came along, I almost changed my mind," she said as they both laughed in unison, thinking of the pains of childbirth.

"Sarah," Patricia told her once the room had become silent once again, "this is so overwhelming to Frank and I. You have a large family. We only have Ben.

If we did anything to destroy our relationship, it would kill us both. The whole thing makes me extremely uncomfortable. Frank and I will talk about it after you leave and reach a decision. However it turns out, I think you and your mother are two extraordinary people."

Mrs. Davis called everyone and they sat down for lunch. Mr. Davis blessed the food and they broke bread together. Sarah noticed that Mr. and Mrs. Davis made sure that she and her aunt were included in the conversations at the table. They tried not to make them feel uncomfortable. As it got closer to their time of departure, Sarah and Aunt Lillian excused themselves to change for their flight home. Ben insisted on going to the airport to assist with everything.

"Ben, they don't have any luggage," Mr. Davis told him.

"I'll go anyway," Ben said with a shrug. "I can keep you company on your way back home."

"Ben," Sarah asked, "Do you have a picture of your family?"

"I wouldn't go anywhere without them. Would you like to see them?" he asked as he found the pictures in his wallet and handed them to her.

"Yes," Aunt Lillian and Sarah responded in unison.

"I'll show you a picture of my family," Sarah offered.

"Is this your husband, Sarah?" Ben asked as he studied her photo.

"Yes, this is my husband, John, and these are our sons and daughters and their children."

"You certainly have a large family."

"Is this your wife?" she asked.

"Yes, this is my wife, Beverly, and this is Christopher and Catrina, our son and daughter and these are our grandchildren."

When they arrived at the airport, Ben wished them a safe flight home. Sarah and Aunt Lillian wished him continued success on his quest to find the cure for AIDS. Aunt Lillian thanked Mr. Davis for their kindness and generosity. "Tell Patricia I said thanks for everything," she told him. She and Sarah then turned and walked into the airport to catch their flight home.

On board the plane, Aunt Lillian said to Sarah, "It's in their hands now. They sure did a fine job raising Ben. Through these difficult circumstances, he was blessed with loving parents."

Sarah looked out over the wing of the plane and lost herself in the cloud formations. They were so lovely, dressed in pastel colors. They looked soft like cotton. It seemed as if one could lie down on the clouds and just float above all of the problems in life.

The flight was smooth. It seemed as if they were suspended in space. She was caught up in the beauty of God's creation. She looked across the sky and thought about how beautiful it was. She was brought back to awareness by Aunt Lillian's voice.

"Did you hear what I said?" she asked Sarah.

"No, I'm sorry. I was thinking about how the clouds are today."

"They are beautiful, aren't they?"

When the plane landed at the airport, Aunt Lillian was beginning to show signs of exhaustion. She asked Sarah to assist her to the front of the airport. Sarah helped her through the airport and then went to bring the car around front. As they drove home, Aunt Lillian admitted that it had been an exhausting day.

"I'm going to get me something to eat and go to bed."

"I'm going to read for a while," Sarah told her. She got her favorite book and started to read. She tried to concentrate on the book, but couldn't. All of the recent events were playing out in her mind. So many things had changed in her life. She wondered if she would ever see Ben again. She wondered what his family was like.

"Lord," she said in desperation, "only you can straighten this out." She drifted off to sleep and woke up around 10 p.m. Aunt Lillian was still asleep in her room. Sarah looked in on her before retiring for the evening.

As she stood in the doorway of Aunt Lillian's room, she thought of what a remarkable woman she was. 'Out of all the adversity she's suffered because of that terrible night, she went to great lengths to protect her two children,' Sarah thought. If nothing else came out of this, she at least had learned the truth about her family tree. 'Lord,' she thought, 'if I can't have all of my family together, I'll settle for that.' She closed the door, went to her room, and went to sleep.

The next morning when Sarah woke up, Aunt Lillian was seated at the kitchen table drinking a cup of coffee.

"You're up early this morning," Sarah told her as she walked into the kitchen.

"I went to bed early last night so I decided to make breakfast this morning," Aunt Lillian responded. "I know you'll be leaving soon. I'd better get back into my routine. I realize this visit has changed our lives forever. When you get old, you look back on your life and wish you could change things. I have often thought of how our lives would have been if things were the way they were supposed to be. I've felt so trapped by my past. Sarah," she continued, "I sure have enjoyed you. Before you leave here, I want you to know that I have willed everything to you. I have been very successful in my business affairs, not like in my personal life. I invested well. Your name is on all of my papers as my beneficiary. If anything happens to me, go straight to my safety deposit box. All the papers and information that you need are in it. I've made some mistakes, but I tried to do the right thing for you and Ben."

"I know you did, Aunt Lillian. Sometimes, things in life aren't easy. We have to live life under the circumstances we find ourselves until we can do better. You've done wonderfully with your life. You don't have anything to feel ashamed of. I hope someday that everyone involved will be able to accept things as they are and learn to love and appreciate each other. Are we going to the funeral tomorrow?"

"I really don't want to," Aunt Lillian answered. "We've done all we can. I don't see how attending the old bastard's funeral is going to help."

"I suppose you're right," Sarah agreed. "Would you like to go to the museum tomorrow?"

"No, I think I'm going to take it easy tomorrow. I feel a little tired from the plane trip to Detroit and back."

For most of the morning, they talked about past memories of the family. They looked through the many picture albums that Aunt Lillian had carefully maintained over the years. They were amazed how much everyone had changed.

"God has been good to this family," Aunt Lillian said. "He brought us out of all of our dilemmas. There are so many struggles behind these pictures. I sure have had my share in my lifetime. I'm so glad you came to visit me. For the first time since that awful night, I feel free. Thanks for coming to help me Sarah."

The telephone rang. "I'll get it," Sarah volunteered. "Hello," she called.

"Hello, is this Lillian?" Mrs. Davis asked.

"No, this is Sarah. Would you like to speak with her?"

"Yes, I would Sarah. This is Pat."

"Just one moment, I'll get her." Sarah didn't know what to expect from this conversation. She went to get Aunt Lillian and then sat down to listen.

"Hi, Patricia. How are you this morning?" Aunt Lillian asked.

"We're both just fine, physically, but emotionally we're distraught. Lillian, we talked about your visit yesterday. We discussed it back and forth all night. Lillian, I'm sorry, but we decided not to tell Ben. We're so afraid of losing him. We want to do the right thing, but we're afraid. Please try to understand the position we're in. Ben and his family are all that we have. If we lose them, I don't believe we could survive the emotional hurt we would have to endure."

"I understand," Aunt Lillian answered. "I respect your decision. Please forgive us for the intrusion on your lives. We won't discuss it again."

Aunt Lillian hung up the phone and looked at Sarah. "I understand," Sarah sighed as she wiped away her tears. Aunt Lillian walked over to Sarah and put her arms around her shoulders.

"Honey," she said, "things don't always turn out the way we would like them to. We must accept their decision."

"We came so close, didn't we Aunt Lillian?"

"Yes, we did," Aunt Lillian responded. "I guess it just wasn't meant to be." They carefully put away the picture albums.

"I did at least get to meet Ben even if I never see him again," Sarah rationalized. She went to her room and began packing for her trip home. Aunt Lillian hated to see her leave, but she knew the time was nearing for her to go. Aunt Lillian followed her into her room.

"I know you're disappointed," she told Sarah. "You still have a wonderful family who loves you. Concentrate on what you have, not what you don't have."

"I know you're right, Aunt Lillian. I'll be fine."

"Are you going by plane or train, Sarah?"

"By plane," Sarah answered. "I'll get home faster. I'm anxious to see John."

The next morning Sarah finished packing. Aunt Lillian was in the kitchen sipping on a cup of coffee. Sarah went into the kitchen and sat down at the table. Aunt Lillian grabbed her hand and bowed her head as she began to pray.

"Lord," she said, "thank you for sending Sarah to free me from my past. Please watch over her as she returns home."

"Do you want someone to take you to the airport?"

"No, Aunt Lillian, you don't have to do that. I'll take a taxi."

"What time do you leave?"

"My flight leaves at 10:30 a.m. I have to be at the gate by 10 a.m. I called John last night. He's going to meet me at the gate in Atlanta. He told me to give you his regards and to ask you to come home with me and visit for a while."

"Sarah, I'm not ready to go right now. I need some time to myself. Maybe I'll come for Thanksgiving."

SARAH'S FLIGHT HOME

The taxi arrived a 9 a.m. Sarah took her bags to the car and returned to the front door where Aunt Lillian was standing. They gave each other a long hug and said goodbye. Sarah turned and started walking toward the taxi. Turning back toward Aunt Lillian, she said, "I love you Aunt Lillian," and blew her a kiss. She got into the taxi and looked out the window until she couldn't see Aunt Lillian anymore. 'I sure would like to see my whole family together before I leave this world,' she thought.

When she arrived at the airport, she checked her bags and walked to the departure gate to check-in. The gate attendant couldn't locate her reservation in the computer. Sarah told her she didn't understand. "I made a reservation through ATTA air travel agency. I checked my bags out front. They must have a reservation in the computer. Can you check with them?" she asked. "I was told at the time I made the reservation that the ticket would be at the departure gate." The gate attendant called baggage check and confirmed Sarah's flight number, but for some strange reason, it was not in her computer.

Sarah called the travel agency to inform them of her dilemma. She was assured that she would be on the flight home. The gate attendant announced flight #526 was ready for boarding. Sarah was afraid she was going to miss the flight. After the last person had boarded, Sarah went to the gate attendant in a final attempt to board the plane. The gate attendant told Sarah they hadn't received confirmation, but she was going to let her on the flight and work everything out with the travel agency. She notified the pilot that there would be one more passenger coming aboard.

Sarah couldn't understand what had happened. She didn't want John worrying about what had happened to her if the flight arrived without her. When she was seated, she fastened her seatbelt and prepared for takeoff. The pilot welcomed everyone aboard flight #526. He told them the ETA at Hartsfield

Airport in Atlanta was about two hours and 15 minutes. The flight attendants gave the passengers their safety instructions and emergency procedures. As they taxied to the runway, Sarah thought how wonderful it would be to get home.

The day was cloudy and overcast. The pilot informed the passengers of a thunderstorm in the area. About an hour into the flight, the "fasten seatbelt" sign came on. The captain assured them that it was just a precaution and there was no need to be alarmed. "We can't get completely above the storm so we're going to experience some turbulence as a result. Will all passengers please return to your seat and fasten your seatbelt?"

The plane began shaking. "Please remain calm," the pilot advised. "We should exit this weather shortly," he said. A few minutes later, he repeated his request for the passengers to remain seated with their seatbelts fastened.

'The weather seems to be getting worse,' Sarah thought. "Oh Lord," she said, "please help us." Lightning bolts lit the sky and thunder cracked all around them. Then, the airplane lost all power and the passenger cabin became eerily dark.

The cabin erupted into chaos as some of the passengers screamed. The flight attendants could barely be heard as they informed the passengers to prepare for an emergency landing. The passengers panicked. Sarah was frightened by all of the chaos and screaming around her. The airplane began a steep decline and crashed into the side of the mountain. When the plane left the radar screen, a search and rescue was implemented immediately.

Aunt Lillian was watching one of her favorite daytime soap operas when it was interrupted by a special news report. A plane had gone down in a heavily wooded area thought to be on the side of a mountain somewhere in Tennessee. "The flight was believed to be flight #526 that originated in Chicago, IL en route to Atlanta, GA. We will update you on this plane crash as soon as information is available," the anchorwoman announced. Then, the station went to a commercial.

"Oh my God," Aunt Lillian gasped. "I wonder if that's the flight Sarah was on. She was supposed to have taken flight #526 into Atlanta."

She immediately tried to call John to verify Sarah's flight number. When she didn't get an answer, she realized that John would have had to leave at the same time the flight left Chicago in order to be there when it arrived. Just then, the news report came back on.

"The flight originated out of Chicago," the anchorwoman repeated. "No one has reached the crash site so we have no reports on survivors or fatalities.

The airline should release a list of passengers shortly. Stay tuned to this station for further information."

Aunt Lillian knew in her heart that this was the flight Sarah was supposed to have taken to Atlanta. She immediately called the airline to try to secure a copy of the passenger list. All the lines were busy. She kept trying until she got through. She explained who she was and requested a copy of the passenger list. She was asked for Sarah's full name and what name she would be flying under. Aunt Lillian gave the information.

"I don't see her name on the passenger list," the representative responded.

"Thank God," Aunt Lillian said and hung up.

Moments later, John called. He was very distraught and wanted to know if Sarah had made her flight. Aunt Lillian calmed him down and told him that she had called the airline and Sarah's name wasn't on the passenger list. Confused, John asked if he could speak to Sarah.

"She isn't here," Aunt Lillian replied.

"Where is she?" he asked.

"I don't know."

"Do you think she's at the airport?"

"I assume that's where she is or she could have caught another flight to Atlanta at the last minute," she proposed.

"How can we find out?" John asked as his mind went into overdrive. He had to find his wife.

"You check the incoming flights from Chicago to Atlanta and I'll call the airlines to see if they had any other flights leaving for Atlanta," she told John. "Call me back in 30 minutes."

John agreed and hung up. Aunt Lillian called the airline to see if they had any other flights leaving for Atlanta since 10:15 a.m. She was informed that they had not. The next flight, they told her, would leave at 1:15 p.m.

"Sarah, where are you?" Aunt Lillian asked out loud. "If you weren't on the plane and you haven't called me or John to let us know you're all right, where can you be?" A few minutes later, the phone rang. John told Aunt Lillian that he had checked the other flights coming in from Chicago. He had also had Sarah paged, but there was no response.

"Have you heard from her?" he asked.

"No, I haven't heard anything. The next flight leaves for Atlanta at 1:15 p.m. John, I don't know where she is," Aunt Lillian whispered as tears began to fill her eyes.

"I'm afraid something has happened to Sarah," he told her.

"Now John," Aunt Lillian cautioned, speaking as much to herself as she was to him, "don't jump to conclusions."

"Did she make her reservations with the airline or through the travel agency?"

"John, I really don't know. She didn't discuss it with me. Do you know which travel agency she would have used?"

"The one we always use is ATTA. Hold on a moment," he said as he shuffled around a bit. "I think I have their card in my wallet. Here it is, Aunt Lillian." John gave Aunt Lillian the telephone number.

"Give me the number where you are and I'll call you back," she said. She was so nervous she could barely make the call. Her hands shook as she dialed the numbers. When the agency answered the phone, Aunt Lillian explained who she was and asked if Sarah Goodwin had made reservations through the agency for flight #526 which had crashed. She was placed on hold for a moment as the customer service representative checked the records. That minute seemed like an hour to Aunt Lillian. Finally, the lady told her that there had been a mix-up that almost kept

Mrs. Goodwin from boarding the flight, but she had been allowed to board at the last minute.

"Oh God," Aunt Lillian gasped.

"I'm so sorry," the lady told her. "If you want to be sure, you can call the departure gate. I'm sure they would remember her," the woman informed her before Aunt Lillian hung up.

As she searched for the number to the airport, she began crying uncontrollably. She had to dial three times before she got the number right. She was barely able to calm herself before getting through. She told the attendant who she was and asked if they remembered a Sarah Goodwin boarding flight # 526. They told her they did not. Aunt Lillian explained about the mix-up at the travel agency and informed them that the travel agency believed she might have boarded at the last minute. The attendant informed Aunt Lillian that she had just recently come on duty.

"Let me check for you," the woman offered. When the attendant came back to the phone, she told Aunt Lillian that she was sorry. "Miss, I hate to tell you this. She was on the flight that went down." Aunt Lillian was so devastated that she dropped the receiver.

As a busy signal blared through the phone a few minutes later, she realized that she had to call John. She picked the phone up from the floor and called him.

"John," she said as calmly as she could, "did someone come with you to the airport?"

"Yes, why Aunt Lillian?"

"May I speak with them?"

"Sarah was on that plane, wasn't she?" he asked her.

"Yes, John, she was."

The receiver tumbled to the floor as she heard John go into hysterics. "Sarah!" he shouted over and over as he sank to his knees. Charlie, John's neighbor, grabbed John with one hand and the receiver with the other. As he held the receiver to his ear, Aunt Lillian told him what had happened and asked him to try to calm John down.

"I'll do my best," he replied with tears in his eyes. "You know how much they care for each other."

"We won't know Sarah's condition until we have more information," Aunt Lillian reminded him, trying to keep a level head through all of the commotion. "I'll call and notify the children. Please take care of John until his family arrives," she told him before she gave him her telephone number should he need to reach her.

"I'll do my best," Charlie promised and hung up.

The next news report came about 5 minutes later. Aunt Lillian had waited for more information before calling the children. The news report indicated a large number of fatalities. There were some survivors, but no identification had been made. They were trying to get medical personnel onto the site before nightfall, but the rescue efforts were being hampered by heavy rainfall in the area. They were also airlifting military personnel with camping equipment so they could set up camp to care for the injured.

Aunt Lillian called John Jr. He was hard to reach because he was in a business meeting. She insisted on speaking with him and told his secretary that it was an emergency. When he finally came to the phone, he asked Aunt Lillian what was wrong.

"I have some bad news," she told him.

"What is it?" he asked.

"Your mother was on the plane that crashed in Tennessee this morning."

"Oh my God!" he gasped. "Is she alive? Is she okay?"

"I don't know. There are survivors, but they haven't released any names."

"Have you spoken with dad?" he asked.

"Your father is at the airport in Atlanta. He was waiting for Sarah's flight to land. He's taking it pretty hard. Charlie is with him. This is the telephone number I have to reach him. John, Jr., you have to be strong for the rest of your family. When you tell them about the crash, make sure you tell them that there are survivors. We can only pray that Sarah is alive," she said.

"Mother always told us to keep our spiritual affairs in order," he reflected. "I'll notify my brothers and sisters, Aunt Lillian."

"I suggest someone get to Atlanta to be with your father as soon as possible," she said before John Jr. hung up.

He decided to call Rebecca first. She was a strong-willed woman, like her mother. When she answered the phone, he told her that he had some bad news.

"John, it's about mother and the plane crash, isn't it?" she asked.

"Yes, it is. Did you hear it on the television?" he asked her.

"Yes, I did. I knew mother was taking flight #526 to Atlanta this morning. She called me before she left Chicago. I turned the television on just before you called and saw the report about the crash."

"Can you call Terry, Jimmie, and Mary to let them know what has happened?"

"Yes, John, I will."

"I'll call Melanie, Thomas, and Robert to let them know if they haven't heard by now. Some of us need to go to Atlanta to be with dad and the rest should head to Tennessee to see about mom. I'll be in touch," he said.

Rebecca took a minute to gain her composure. Her hands shook as she decided to call Mary first. She couldn't reach her. She left a message with her answering service. She remembered the Caribbean cruise Mary had planned to take. She was probably aboard the fantasy cruise ship. She called the cruise line and found out that her sister's ship was supposed to dock in Fort Lauderdale in two days. She was given the ship's telephone number and she called and left a message for Mary to call as soon as possible. She then called Terry. He was home setting up his office. He had been laid off his job about three months ago so he had decided to go into business for himself. When he answered the phone, Rebecca said, "Terry, I'm so glad you're there."

"Is this Rebecca?" he asked.

"Yes, it's me, Terry."

"What's wrong? You sound upset."

"Mama was on flight #526 that went down in Tennessee this morning."

"Did she survive the crash?" he asked as his heart dropped.

"We don't know. The airline hasn't released the names of the survivors." Rebecca could hear him breathing deeply.

"Where is daddy?" he asked.

"He's at the airport in Atlanta. He's there with Charlie. He'll be all right until some of us get there. I'll leave right away for Atlanta to be with him." Before she could hang up, Jimmie called.

"What flight was mother taking to Atlanta?" he asked.

"Oh Jimmie," she sighed, "she was on flight #526 that went down."

"I had a feeling she was on that flight," he sighed. "Have they released the names of any survivors?"

"All I know is that there are survivors," she said. "Are you all right, Jimmie?"

"No, I'm not all right. I feel like I'm going to explode inside, but I guess I'll manage. I'm catching the first plane to Tennessee."

A few moments later, Mary called. "Becca, you should be here with me! This place is really gorgeous," Mary told Rebecca excitedly.

"Mary, mother was on flight #526 that crashed in Tennessee this morning," Rebecca told her. As Mary listened to her sister, her excitement turned to shock. There was complete silence. Rebecca heard a man's voice in the background asking her sister if she was okay. She heard the man pick up the receiver and say hello.

"Who is this?" Rebecca asked.

"My name is Paul, I'm traveling with Mary."

"What happened to her?" Rebecca asked. Her heart was pounding. She wished she could have told her sister in person. At least she would have been there to comfort her.

"I believe she fainted."

"I'm her sister, Rebecca. Our mother was on a plane that crashed today. I just gave her the news. That's probably why she fainted. Can you make sure she's okay and tell her to call me when she's feeling better?"

On the other side of the country, John Jr. was calling Thomas. Thomas had become quite an outdoors man since returning home from the war. He had organized a company that trained and furnished tour guides for people wanting to hike along the Appalachian Trail. John could not reach him. Thomas was out with a group of hikers and he was scheduled to return today, if the weather didn't delay him and his group. He left an urgent message for him to call immediately.

Robert was next to be called. He was a college professor. He was a very intelligent man who had written several books, two of which had made the Bestseller's List. He was also an accomplished public speaker. He was the intellect of the family.

When John reached him, he was getting ready to teach a class on public speaking. He was ecstatic to hear little John's voice. Sarah was sure that Robert would be called to preach the gospel some day. She thought his voice just resonated through a crowd of people.

"Robert, I have bad news. Mother was on flight #526 that crashed in Tennessee this morning."

"Holy Jesus," Robert replied. He had not been expecting such news. Bracing himself for what else John had to say, he sat down slowly, leaning against his desk. His hands began to sweat as he gripped the phone.

"There are survivors. We don't know if she's one of them or not."

Robert told John Jr. he was cancelling his itinerary and flying immediately to Tennessee. After he hung up, Rebecca called John and told him that Mary fainted when she heard what happened. "She called me back a few minutes ago and told me that her friend, Paul, is flying with her to be with dad."

"I haven't called Melanie," John Jr. said. "I was unable to reach Thomas. He's hiking along the Appalachian Trail and is supposed to return today. I left an urgent message for him to call. I'll call Melanie as soon as we hang up," he said.

Of all the Goodwin siblings, Melanie was the most emotional. She had worked very hard to become a lawyer and took cases that she knew some of her clients could not pay her for. She insisted that everyone was entitled to good legal representation. She reminded her critics that money shouldn't be the only motivation one should have for choosing a career or profession. Helping mankind should also be included.

John Jr. thought she would take the news very hard. After explaining things to her, she didn't respond as he thought she would.

"John" she said, "God will bring us through this. Where do you want me to go?" she asked.

"Go to Atlanta and be with Dad. Some of us will join you there. This is the number you can reach me with. I haven't been able to reach Thomas," John said.

"Thanks, brother. I'll leave right away," she said.

THE SEARCH FOR SARAH

The rescue team reached the crash site and began to establish a command post. They erected tents and installed a generator so they would have a shelter for the night. The rescuers had started searching for the survivors and were trying to locate them before nightfall. They had succeeded in rescuing some of the survivors before it became too dark. The search would be resumed the next morning at daybreak.

The next morning, the names of the ones that had been rescued were released. Sarah's name was not on the list. The news report indicated that there might be more survivors. Sarah's family was saddened, but hopeful that she would be found alive.

Aunt Lillian was about to go out of her mind with worry. She had to talk to someone. She picked up the phone and began dialing the first number that came to mind. The voice on the other end said hello. Aunt Lillian, not knowing whom she had dialed, asked to whom she was speaking.

"This is Patricia Davis. You have reached the Davis residence."

Aunt Lillian fell apart. She started crying into the phone. Patricia could barely understand her.

"Patricia, this is Lillian."

"What's wrong, Lillian?" Patricia asked her, alarmed.

"I didn't know whom I had dialed. Sarah left for Atlanta this morning and the plane she was on went down."

"Is this the same flight that has been on television all day?"

"Yes, that's the one," Aunt Lillian said as she made an attempt to pull herself together. She grabbed a few tissues and wiped her face and nose.

"Oh my goodness. Jesus, Jesus, did she survive?"

"We don't know. Her name wasn't on the list. I'm praying they will find her alive tomorrow."

"I'm so sorry about the crash. Our prayers are with you. If there's anything we can do, please let us know."

"I appreciate your concern. I had to talk to someone." Feeling relieved, but awkward, Aunt Lillian thanked her and said good night.

At dawn, the rescue team resumed working at the crash site. They removed all the passengers from the plane. Some of them were identified right away. They also found more survivors and airlifted them to receive medical treatment.

While the different sections of the plane were being examined, they found the black box that recorded the conversation of the pilots. They sent it in immediately so they could determine what happened. They believed the storm was the cause of the plane crash, but they would not know for sure until they examined the black box. The rescue was proving to be very difficult because of the mountain terrain.

The plane had crashed into Clansman Dome, the highest peak in the Great Smoky Mountains and a part of the Appalachian Trail. All the passengers were being airlifted to Knoxville for hospitalization and identification.

Jimmie, Robert, and Rebecca arrived in Knoxville and checked into the Holiday Inn. Terry, Mary, Melanie, and John Jr. checked into the Atlanta Hilton Hotel with John. They decided to wait there until they heard about Sarah's condition. Around 2 p.m., more names were released. Again, Sarah's name was not on the list. Three of the survivors, a man and two women, had not been identified. They were unconscious, but they were alive.

On the morning of the crash, Thomas and his hikers had heard something that sounded like a loud explosion echo through the mountains. He and his hikers were entering the state of Tennessee from North Carolina. They couldn't determine what it was at the time. He told the group that it was common to hear strange things along the trail.

As they continued their hike into Tennessee, they began seeing large pieces of debris scattered along the trail. At first, it appeared to be clothing and pieces of luggage. Thomas became very concerned. Of all the years of hiking the trail, he had never encountered anything like this. He examined some of it as they walked along.

Up ahead of him, he could see a large piece of metal. It looked like part of the wing of an aircraft. He suddenly realized what the loud noise they had heard was. An airplane had crashed into the mountain.

When they got closer, they could see the crash site. There was a burned area where the plane had gone down. Thomas could hear people moving about and talking. He and his group began making their way down the side of the mountain toward the crash site.

Jimmie, Robert, and Rebecca became very discouraged when they learned their mother's name was not on the list of survivors. They were informed of three or four passengers that had not been found. "We should find them all before nightfall," they were told.

About 400 yards up the mountain, Thomas began hearing voices crying for help. At first, the group thought it was the wind going among the trees. They continued their descent and the voices became clearer.

They first located two women and a man. Thomas removed his first-aid kit and started dressing the lacerations and bruises on the man. He appeared to have a broken leg. The other members of the group attended to the women. They prepared them the best they could and started moving them toward the campsite.

About a hundred yards from where they had found the first three passengers, the group saw a woman sitting on the ground with her back against a tree. Her face was bruised and lacerated and the front of her dress and blouse were stained with blood.

When they got closer, they could hear her calling for help. Thomas was too far away to hear her voice. He continued down the mountain toward the campsite while two of the hikers went over to her and rendered her aid.

As they touched her shoulder, she reached up, her hands shaking terribly, and allowed them to help her to her feet. "Thank you father," she said as they pulled her up. Before they could steady her, she lost consciousness. One of the two hikers gently lifted her and carried her down the mountain.

Jimmie, Robert, and Rebecca decided to call their father in Atlanta to let him know what was going on in Knoxville. They knew he was listening to the news reports, but they wanted to keep him informed personally. They told John all of the passengers had been accounted for except four. The last report they had received said all passengers should be located before nightfall.

"They indicated that if the passengers are not located before nightfall, they might not survive another night in the woods. Some of the passengers who lost lives in the crash haven't been identified. Some are in such bad condition that they will have to be identified by dental records or by some other means," Rebecca informed him.

"I don't believe Sarah is dead. I think she is alive. She's hurt, but she's alive," John told her.

"I hope you're right."

John Jr. decided to call Aunt Lillian to keep her informed. She was so very glad he called. She asked if Sarah had been found and if she was all right. John Jr. told Aunt Lillian that Sarah had not been found, but they were still hopeful that she was alive.

"Dad believes she is still alive."

"Your father and mother are very close. He feels something in his soul and that's why he feels that way. God works in mysterious ways. His wonders he performs. Tell everyone to keep the faith and keep praying for her," Aunt Lillian said.

The closer Thomas got to the crash site, the more it reminded him of the war in Vietnam. He had a very strange feeling, as if the crash site had been bombed. There were civilians and military personnel going through the wreckage. When members of the rescue team saw Thomas and the hikers exit the woods, they went to meet them. They carried the wounded passengers to the medical tent and asked Thomas who he was and where he had found the passengers. They offered him and his group something to drink and told Thomas and his group that these were the remaining four passengers of flight #526.

"How many were on board?" Thomas asked him.

"There were 165 passengers aboard. Only 11 survived the crash".

"The lady your group brought in unconscious is still alive. If she makes it, she is number 11. The rescue part of the mission is over. All the passengers have been accounted for and we are airlifting all of them out before nightfall. We should be able to finish our investigation in two or three more days."

"What caused the crash?" Thomas asked.

"We don't know for certain," the man answered him. "There was a terrible electrical storm in the flight path. We believe it fouled up the instrument panel causing the plane to lose power. The pilot probably thought he was above the mountains. Where are you and your group headed?"

"Knoxville," Thomas replied, thinking of the long trip home. After the surprise of finding a crash site, he was not looking forward to the journey.

"We certainly appreciate your help. You are welcome to board the helicopters for Knoxville if you like."

"If there's anything more we can do to help you, please let us know. This is my first time seeing a commercial airline crash site. I'm going to talk to the group and see if they want to board the helicopter," Thomas said.

"Sir, I've seen too many of them. Sometimes, I have nightmares about them."

After Thomas spoke with the group they decided to take the helicopter. Many were saddened because of what they saw at the crash site. Thomas was reminded of how he lost his leg and a very close friend in the Vietnam war. He informed the man that they would take him up on his offer to take the helicopter to Knoxville. They were the last to leave the crash site along with the rescue team.

Thomas had always found peace and contentment hiking through the Appalachians. The mountains always posed challenges that helped make one stronger and appreciate the wonders of the mountains.

Viewing the crash site from above, he was reminded how unforgiving the mountains can be. They were so massive, it was almost like they defied one to take the adventure of a lifetime. Once taken, most people returned again and again.

The mountains could never be mastered, its challenges simply had to be accepted. 'You learn to coexist with them as you explore its many wonders,' he thought. 'In a few months the scars from the crash will disappear and become part of the natural wonders of this majestic chain of nature.'

Upon their arrival in Knoxville, Thomas and his group secured taxicabs and went to the Holiday Inn. Thomas checked in, shaved, and took a long hot shower. He went to the restaurant to get something to eat before checking with his office.

When he arrived at the restaurant, Thomas thanked the Lord for another safe journey through the mountains. From where he sat, he could see guests passing in the hallway as they made their way to and from the main entrance where the elevators were located. While he was giving thanks to the Lord, Jimmie, Robert, and Rebecca passed by in route to the hospital where the survivors of flight #526 were hospitalized. He had his head bowed and missed them by seconds.

Thomas' meal was delicious. His taste buds tingled as he savored every bite. He finished his meal and returned to his room to check in with his office. After placing the call, he didn't get an answer. He tried his voice mail to get his messages.

"Thomas, I hope you had a safe trip," he heard his secretary say. "The Freeman group is ready to finalize plans for their hike. Another group wants to talk to you personally about a trip through the mountains. It seems like you're going to be a very busy man. Oh, by the way, your brother John called. He said it was urgent that you get in touch with him as soon as possible."

Thomas smiled after hearing the message from John Jr., but he was concerned about the urgency of his message. Thomas called John Jr.'s home, but didn't get an answer. He called his parent's home to touch base with them. He didn't get an answer there either. He decided he would place the calls again just before he went to bed.

He went and filled his ice bucket and started back to his room. As he passed one of the elevators, the doors opened and Rebecca, Jimmie, and Robert stepped out. Rebecca turned and looked in Thomas' direction as they were walking away. She saw his back and thought, 'Is that Thomas?' She knew it was him by his limp and immediately called to him. He turned around to see who called his name and was surprised to see Rebecca, Robert, and Jimmie. Rebecca ran and hugged his neck, telling him how glad she was that he was there.

"I'm glad to see all of you too. What are you doing here? What's with the serious faces?"

"You haven't heard?" Robert asked.

"Are you talking about the plane crash?" he asked, not understanding why it would have affected them so profoundly.

"Yes," Robert responded. "My group and I came across the crash site this morning. Matter-of-fact, we were the ones who found that last four survivors," he explained.

"Did you see mother out there?" Rebecca asked, hopeful that her mother had at last been found.

"What do you mean?" Thomas asked as alarm bells started going off in his head. 'Had their mother been on that plane?' he thought.

"She was on the flight."

As Thomas heard Rebecca's words, he dropped his ice bucket. Ice slid across the floor in various directions. "Is she alive?" he asked as his hands began to tremble.

"We don't know. We haven't been able to determine if she's in the hospital."

"Are you okay, Thomas?" Robert asked. His brother's face had turned ashen and pale.

"I'll be all right. This is quite a shock. We almost lost dad, now this. I wonder what will happen next."

Thomas and his mother had a very close relationship. She was the one whom he could talk to about his problems when he returned from the war. When he was young, his brothers and sisters used to call him mama's boy because of his relationship with his mother. Robert and Jimmie stood by his side to support him should he need it.

"The crash site is terrible. It reminds me of the war. We came across two women and a man about 400 yards from the crash site."

"Did you get a good look at the women?"

"Yes I did. Neither one was mother. When we reached the crash site, we were told that the four that we found were the last remaining passengers of the flight. All of the other passengers had been accounted for."

"You said four, the last remaining four. Did you get a good look at the fourth passenger you found?" Robert asked.

"No, I didn't. I didn't see her or know about her until we reached the crash site. Her face was bandaged. She had cuts and lacerations that seemed to be pretty severe. She lost consciousness before she reached the crash site. She is the only one that I didn't get a look at. If all the passengers have been accounted for and mom's not one of the fatalities, that must be her."

They decided to go back to the hospital. The lady they believed was their mother had been admitted as one of the survivors. When they arrived, they were told that Sarah's name was not on the list. Rebecca asked if they had admitted anyone who had not been identified. She was told that there were two, a man and a woman. They were hospitalized in the intensive care unit. The woman had been unconscious upon admission.

"Does she have lacerations and bandages on her face?"

"Yes, her face was bandaged when she arrived here. Those have been removed and replaced with new ones."

"May we see her? We believe she's our mother, Sarah Goodwin."

"She is in a serious, but stable condition. The doctors are very concerned about her. A team of specialists is with her now. Please, be patient a little while longer. She is getting the best of care. All of the survivors are. If this is your mother, the only thing you can do is pray."

Rebecca politely asked the nurse if she could go into the intensive care unit and do something for her. The nurse agreed that if it was within reason, she'd do it.

"Would you please go and look on her left hand and see if there's a diamond and ruby ring on her finger? It has an S in the center."

Rebecca had given her mother the ring on Mother's Day. She hoped it hadn't come off during the crash. The nurse went to go see.

"When are we going to call dad?" Robert asked.

"I think we need to wait until the nurse returns so that we can be reasonably sure this lady is mom," Rebecca said.

It took the nurse about 15 minutes before returning to give her report. As she walked back, she began to smile. She told them that the lady did have a diamond and ruby ring with an S in the center. "I believe this is your mother."

"Praise the Lord, our prayers have been answered. Mother is alive!" Rebecca exclaimed. She'd had that ring specially made for her mother. The chances of someone else having it were very remote.

Jimmie called their father and told him of the good news. They were certain this lady was Sarah. They told him how they were able to make the identification with the ring Rebecca gave her on Mother's Day. He was told that Thomas had come across the crash site with the group he was hiking with and his group was responsible for finding the last four passengers that survived the crash. Unbeknown to him, his mother was one of the people his group had found. He was told that she was unconscious and had been since she was rescued. She and the rest of the survivors were receiving the very best of care. She was listed in serious but stable condition. When John heard the news, he thanked God that Sarah was alive.

"I'll tell the rest of the family the good news. We'll be leaving for Knoxville right away." After informing the family, John went into the restroom and cried. He did not want his family to see him cry. He felt so helpless. He was unable to help Sarah. All he could do was ask the Lord to take care of her.

John Jr. called Aunt Lillian to tell her the good news. When she answered the phone John Jr. said, "Aunt Lillian, I have some wonderful news."

"Sarah is alive, isn't she?"

"Yes, she is alive. She is in the hospital in Knoxville. She is unconscious and listed in serious but stable condition. She was the very last person to be found. Thomas was conducting one of his hiking tours along the Appalachian Trail. He and his group are the ones who found the last four passengers and mom was the last to be found."

"The Lord really does work in mysterious ways, doesn't he?" said Aunt Lillian.

"Yes, he does Aunt Lillian. There is much more I will be able to tell you once we get to Knoxville. We love you Aunt Lillian."

"I love ya'll too," she said.

Aunt Lillian called Patricia Davis to let her know that Sarah had been found alive. She informed her of her condition and asked for her prayers. Mrs. Davis was elated to hear the good news.

"I will relay the message to Mr. Davis. Take care Lillian and keep us informed."

John, John Jr., Mary, Melanie, and Terry arrived in Knoxville at about 10 a.m. the next morning. They went straight to the hospital. After greeting the family, they were told of Sarah's condition. She had improved but was still unconscious. John wanted to see her right away, but was not allowed to until the doctors agreed it would be okay. He asked the nurse how severe the lacerations were to Sarah's face. He was told that they appeared much worst than they actually were.

"She might need plastic surgery. The doctors will determine that later, but she should be okay. This is not uncommon for someone who's been in an accident of this magnitude. The doctors who are treating her believe that she will regain consciousness in a day or two. All of her vital signs are stable and her major organs are functioning properly. We're hopeful that she is going to be just fine. The most important thing she needs right now is time for her body to heal from the shock it has gone through. Come, let me take you to the seventh floor so you can meet Dr. Gray. He's in charge of Mrs. Goodwin's care."

As they made their way to the intensive care unit on the seventh floor, everyone was extremely quiet. They had never seen her in this condition before. Not knowing how they would react, they were afraid that their emotions would get the best of them.

John believed Sarah would recover, but for some strange reason he had an uneasy feeling in his stomach. Sarah had never been seriously injured during their married life. She had gone through so much in the last 48 hours. John had always tried to protect Sarah, but now he knew the only thing he could do for her was to continue to pray.

They arrived on the seventh floor and the nurse told them that Dr. Gray was busy with another patient. It would be a while before he would be able to see them.

When Dr. Gray finally came, he introduced himself to the family. He told John that he was in charge of Sarah's care. John asked him if he believed that she would come out of her coma soon.

"There is no way we can determine when she will emerge from the coma. We hope it will be in a day or two, but it could be longer."

"When can I see Sarah, Dr. Gray?" John asked him.

"Mr. Goodwin, I know you need to see your wife. Let me go back and make sure everything is okay with her. I'll be back shortly."

About 15 minutes later, Dr. Gray returned to the waiting room.

"Mr. Goodwin, I'm going to take you to see your wife, now. I want to prepare you for what you're going to see," he stated as they walked down the corridor. "She is connected to several machines that are monitoring her condition. Her face is bandaged due to the lacerations she received during the crash. She also has cuts and bruises all over her body. Those aren't as serious as the ones on her face. For all practical purposes, she looks as if she is asleep. She won't know that you're there. Please, try to control your emotions while you are with her. Come, Mr. Goodwin, let's go see your wife."

John's heart started pounding. He and Dr. Gray walked to the room and Dr. Gray opened the door to let John enter first. John saw Sarah just as Dr. Gray had described her.

Immediately, he detected a state of peacefulness permeating the room. His heart started beating out of rhythm, but he calmed down after a while. His precious Sarah was lying there, motionless. John walked over to her bedside and touched her hand.

"It's John," he said. "We have finally found you."

He felt her fingers move slightly. He caressed her hand as he told Sarah that everything would be all right. Dr. Gray told John that Sarah could not hear him. Unmoved, John repeated himself, "Sarah, this is John. Don't be afraid. We're here with you." John felt Sarah squeeze his hand slightly. He believed he had made contact with Sarah despite the darkness that was holding her conscious mind captive. After a little while, Dr. Gray told John that it was time for Sarah to be checked by the nurse. "You can visit her later," he promised.

John didn't want to let go of Sarah's hand.

"I must go so the nurse can check you now. I'll be back to see you soon," he promised. John returned to the waiting room where his sons and daughters were anxiously waiting to see what condition he had found their mother in. Before they could say anything, he told them that Sarah would be okay.

"God is watching over her," he told them. Once again, he could see smiles on their faces. "Do you think the doctor will let us see mother?" Rebecca asked.

"I think all of you will get to see her. It's going to take some time though. The doctors are being very careful with Sarah and the rest of the survivors." With that, John walked back to the nurse's station and thanked them for the care they were giving Sarah.

DR. BEN DAVIS ARRIVES IN KNOXVILLE

When John was leaving the nurse's station, he heard a gentleman asking about Sarah's condition. John thought he was one of the doctors caring for the patients in the intensive care unit.

"Are you a doctor?" John asked. Dr. Davis turned around and told him that he was.

"Are you on the hospital staff, sir?" one of the nurses inquired, unfamiliar with his face.

"No, I'm not on staff here."

"Are you one of the specialists sent to examine some of the patients?" she further inquired.

"No," he said. "I'm not here to examine any patients."

"Then, why are you interested in Sarah's condition?" John asked him before the nurse could inquire any further.

"This is Mr. Goodwin," the nurse explained to Dr. Davis.

"I'm pleased to meet you, Mr. Goodwin," Dr. Davis told him, unwilling to offer any additional information on why he was asking about Sarah.

"Who are you?" John asked. "And why are you here?"

"My name is Benjamin Davis. I met your wife in Detroit, Michigan. I'd rather not say anything else. You wouldn't believe me anyway. I'll let Sarah explain everything when she regains consciousness. Hopefully, that won't be too long."

John wondered why Sarah hadn't told him about this doctor. She had gone to Chicago, not Detroit. It wasn't like her to keep secrets. He headed back to the waiting room and asked if anyone knew of a Dr. Benjamin Davis. No one knew him, but they were curious as to why he wanted to know.

"He's at the nurse's station asking about Sarah's condition. He said he met her in Detroit, Michigan."

"But, mama didn't go to Detroit, did she dad?" Thomas asked.

"Your mother went to Chicago. I don't know anything about her going to Detroit. Dr. Davis said that Sarah would have to explain things when she comes out of her coma. He said I wouldn't believe him if he told me," John said.

Determined to get to the bottom of this, Thomas went to the nurse's station to see this doctor, but he wasn't there. The nurse told him that he had left.

All of the Goodwins wanted to know how this man knew their mother. They also wanted to know why he was there. He was not a family member. It was all very perplexing and not at all what the family needed at this particular time.

Dr. Davis returned around 5 p.m. that afternoon to check on Sarah's condition. Nothing had changed. He asked to see her and was informed that only the attending physicians, the nurses, and the family were allowed inside the intensive care unit.

"Are you a family member, sir?" the nurse asked him. Unsure of how to answer the question, given the surprising news he had recently received, Ben looked at her and agreed to wait until Sarah had regained consciousness. He wanted to tell everyone who he was, he wanted to get the answers to his questions, but Sarah was the only one who could provide those answers. He wanted so much and felt so alone. This was his family, but he couldn't tell them and he really didn't know if he'd be able to accept them anyway.

Suddenly, there was a lot of activity in the nurse's station. There seemed to be an emergency. John noticed that everyone was in a hurry. An announcement sounded across the hospital intercom for Dr. Gray to return to the intensive care unit immediately.

John had a feeling something was wrong with Sarah. He went to the nurse's station and asked if something was wrong with his wife. He was told not to worry as the nurses rushed to and fro. They assured him that she would be taken care of if the emergency was related to her. John told his family that he believed something was wrong with Sarah.

"The doctors and nurses are with her."

John was trying to be strong for his family. "Oh, Lord," he said, "I love her so much." The family gathered around and tried to comfort him. At that moment, Ben walked in and saw that something was wrong. Recognizing Sarah's husband, he asked, "Is Sarah okay?"

"Why are you asking questions about our mother?" Thomas asked before his father could respond.

"Look, I don't mean you or your family any harm. If I told you the truth, you wouldn't believe me."

"Why don't you try me and see if I'll believe you or not?"

"I'd rather wait and let your mother tell you."

"Did mother come to Detroit to see you?" Thomas pressed on.

"She didn't exactly come to Detroit to see me."

"But you did see her while she was there…" Thomas replied.

"Yes, I saw her while she was there."

"You are a doctor, aren't you?"

"Yes."

"Was something wrong with her and she didn't want us to know?"

"I can assure you there was nothing wrong with her physically that I know about when she was in Detroit. She didn't come to Detroit to see me as a doctor. She didn't keep any secrets about her health as far as I know." Having had enough, Ben excused himself to check on Sarah.

Ben talked to the nurses and made a telephone call. A few minutes later, he told John and his family that Sarah had shown signs of coming out of the coma. "That is the reason for all the excitement," he explained.

"Our prayers are being answered!" John exclaimed as he lifted his hands in praise. He and his family were very excited to hear the news. "How long do you think it will be before we will be able to see her?" John asked.

"The doctor must analyze her condition mentally and physically to determine when she will be able to receive family members. The most important thing is to keep her vital signs stable so she can continue to recover. Dr. Gray won't keep you from seeing her any longer than is necessary," Ben told them.

"Mr. Goodwin," Dr. Gray said as he entered the waiting room, "will you please excuse

Dr. Davis? I need to speak with him privately."

"Sure," John said as his brow wrinkled in frustration. Dr. Gray had not answered any of his questions, but now he was conversing with this stranger about his wife's condition. He watched as Dr. Davis and Dr. Gray disappeared around the corner.

"What do you need to speak with me about?" Ben asked Dr. Gray.

"I didn't want to say anything in front of Mr. Goodwin. Mrs. Goodwin is doing just fine. She has been calling your name and asking for you. Your first name is Ben, isn't it?"

"Yes, it is."

"She has been asking for you ever since she began speaking. I didn't want to say anything to Mr. Goodwin before speaking with you first. I don't know what is going on with you and her family. It's really none of my business, but the continued progress of Mrs. Goodwin is my concern."

"Dr. Gray, all of my intentions are honorable. There is nothing shady going on," Ben assured him. "I wouldn't do anything to cause stress or harm to the Goodwin family. If I tried to explain why I'm here, I don't think it would be fair to the family because I couldn't make them understand. I'm still having trouble understanding it myself. Hopefully, she'll regain full consciousness soon and, when you think the time is right, she can explain to her family who I am."

"Okay. In the meantime, will you come with me to intensive care?" Dr. Gray asked him.

"Sure, I'd be happy to," Ben agreed.

When Ben saw Sarah, she was resting comfortably with her eyes closed. After a few minutes, she began to call Ben's name. He walked over to her bedside. "Sarah, I'm here," he said.

She continued to call his name. Again Ben assured her of his presence. "Everything is going to be fine," he told her. Sarah paused as if she heard him. Ben continued to speak to her. He could feel her faintly squeeze his hand. 'She knows I'm here,' he thought.

Dr. Gray realized that there was some type of relationship between Sarah and Ben. In a low tone, he heard Ben tell Sarah that John and the rest of the family were waiting to see her.

"We're all waiting on you to get well," he said. "I'll be here as long as it takes."

"That's enough for now," Dr. Gray said softly as he waited for Ben at the door.

When Ben returned to the family, he was immediately questioned by John who had been thinking non-stop since Ben had left the room with Dr. Gray.

"What's going on?"

"I think you need to get Dr. Gray and let him explain," Ben told him. Frustrated, John called for the nurse and asked her to page Dr. Gray. When the doctor came to see the family, he explained that Sarah was talking in a semiconscious state. "She isn't responding to questions, but she is talking. She is coming out of the coma, but it will be a while."

Turning back to Ben, John addressed him. "Dr. Davis," John said, "my family wants to know who you are, but we are willing to wait until Sarah comes around."

Relieved, Ben thanked him. "I would prefer it that way," he said.

The next morning, after having a good night's sleep, John and his family returned to the hospital to check on Sarah. They were elated to learn that she had regained consciousness. With excitement glowing on their faces, they asked how long it would be before they could see her.

"Be careful not to excite her," Dr. Gray warned John "Mrs. Goodwin regained consciousness about one o'clock this morning. She was very talkative and had a lot of questions about you, Dr. Davis, and the rest of the family. She has been asking for you and Dr. Davis. I would like both of you to go in at the same time. I have spoken with her about the accident and she is well aware of what has happened and the extent of her injuries."

'Why is my wife asking for Dr. Davis? Who is he?' John thought. He looked at Dr. Gray as he finished speaking and asked, "Why weren't we notified of her progress?"

"Mr. Goodwin, I made the decision not to notify anyone until I had made my physical examination. I believe I was right in making that decision. At 11 a.m., I want you and Dr. Davis to visit with your wife for a few minutes. She has something she has to tell you. After your visit, I'll decide whether she will be able to see the rest of your family today."

John told his family what Dr. Gray had told him. They were also puzzled as to Dr. Davis' role in this situation. They wondered why their mother had requested to see him.

John asked his family to be patient just a little while longer. "I believe everything will be explained shortly," he told them. "I have to admit, I'm just as puzzled as everyone else, though." Cautioning himself as much as his family, John thought that was the understatement of the year. The tension in the room was growing by the minute. He didn't know if he could control his family's reaction much longer.

When Ben walked into the room, all eyes turned to him. "Good morning," he said. None of them said anything.

"Good morning, Dr. Davis," John said, trying to lead his family by example. Ben could feel the tension in the room.

'Something is wrong,' he thought. "Is something wrong with Sarah?" he asked.

"No, she's just fine, but I'd like to know just who the hell you are!" Thomas exploded.

Thomas had grown increasingly angry throughout this ordeal and not having any answers about Dr. Davis' relationship with his mother was fueling the fire. This mysterious man was getting next to him. "Mom asked to see you before seeing her sons and daughters and I want to know why!" he ground out.

"She's awake?" Ben ventured.

"Yes, she's awake and talking," Thomas returned staring at Ben as if he'd charge him at any moment.

"Thomas, your mother will explain everything we need to know about Dr. Davis. I know tempers are on edge right now because we don't know who he is," John said, trying in earnest to calm his son down. The other visitors in the waiting room had become very quiet and were staring quite openly at the scene. John knew if Thomas did not calm down, they might be asked to leave the hospital. Not to mention how upset and worried Sarah would be if she found out what was going on.

"I know this is a strange circumstance for you and it is for me also. It has been very difficult for you as a family. It has been very difficult for my family as well," Ben attempted to explain. "I wish we could have met under different circumstances, but we didn't. I hope I haven't caused you any harm or pain. If I have, it was not my intention, I assure you. I have only known you for a short period of time, but I can tell there is something very special about this family. I'm making you a promise. Before this day passes, you will know exactly who I am and why I'm here," Ben emotionally explained to the family. 'Lord,' he prayed, 'please let Sarah be able to put their minds at ease.'

John followed Ben out of the room and told him that they were to see Sarah at 11 a.m.

"I'll be glad when this is all over," Ben told him. "I could have told you and your family who I am when I first arrived. I only just found out. If I hadn't waited, I would have confused the situation more than it is right now." As Ben spoke, he wiped his eyes. "Sarah is the one who should tell her family who I am. I can understand why Thomas feels the way he does toward me. I'm sure the others are thinking the same thing, they just haven't said anything."

"Dr. Davis," John told him, "my children are very concerned about their mother. I was in the hospital myself not long ago. I was in a coma, just like my wife was. That's why they are concerned about their mother. Sarah has never kept secrets from me as long as we've been married. I'm confident that there is a good explanation for your being here. I'm not going to say any more about it. I'll let Sarah explain who you are."

At 11 a.m., Dr. Gray came to the waiting room to get John and Ben. He escorted them through the hospital corridor to Sarah's room. Ben's heart was pounding. He didn't know what to expect.

Once outside the room, Dr. Gray warned them not to upset Sarah. Dr. Gray then entered the room and John followed him. Ben was the last to enter.

When the door opened, Sarah was looking out the window. "Mrs. Goodwin," Dr. Gray called to her, "I have someone to see you." Sarah turned in his direction. When she saw John, she smiled as tears began to roll down her cheeks, landing on the pillow under her head. "My prince is here," she said. "I was so afraid I'd never see you again, John."

John walked to the side of the bed. He leaned over and touched her hand. With misty eyes, he said, "I'm so glad you're okay. We thought we had lost you." He kissed her hand. "I love you so much," he told her. "How do you feel, sweetheart?"

"I don't feel like dancing, but I feel okay. How are the children?"

"They're okay. They're all waiting to see you."

"You and I have put them through quite a lot here lately. We've got to stop having our family reunions in hospitals," she told him as they shared a smile.

"Mrs. Goodwin, there is someone else here to see you," Dr. Gray interrupted.

Ben was standing near the door. He walked closer to Sarah. "Hello," he said. "Mom and dad told me after they found out that your flight went down. I had to come and see if there was anything I could do. I'm still confused about a lot of things, but I had to come. I hope my being here hasn't caused your family too much inconvenience."

Sarah began to cry. "We're your family, Ben," she told him. "We're all family. I'm so glad you're here. John," she said as she turned to her husband, "I want you to meet your brother-in-law, Dr. Benjamin Davis."

John was speechless. "Did you say brother-in-law?" he asked.

"Yes, I said brother-in-law," she repeated.

"So, that means he would have to be your brother," John said as he slowly began to try to put the pieces together.

"Yes, John, this is my brother, Ben. I didn't know I had a brother until I arrived in Chicago. I have so much to tell you, honey. I learned so much during my visit to Aunt Lillian."

"Don't try to tell it all now," Dr. Gray cautioned. "You'll have lots of time to talk."

"John, I hope you understand why I wanted Sarah to tell you who I am," Ben said to John, "you never would have believed me."

"You're absolutely right, Ben. I'm still confused about the whole thing," he said, shaking his head in disbelief.

"I'll explain later," Sarah promised him. Sarah then asked Dr. Gray if she could see her children. "They need to see me," she explained. "If only for a short while."

"Okay, Mrs. Goodwin," Dr. Gray agreed. "I'll let them all come in at the same time. They can only stay for a minute or two."

"Thank you. This will give me an opportunity to tell them about Ben. They need to hear it from me."

"I don't usually let this many people in to see a patient in ICU, but I'll make an exception this one time," Dr. Gray explained.

John went to the waiting room and told his family they could go in to see their mother.

"You mean all of us?" Thomas asked.

"Yes, all of you can go in to see her. She's waiting," John said. "Don't all of you talk to her at the same time. We don't want to tire her out. We need to take it slow so she can regain her strength. She looks worse than she really is with the bandages on her face. I'm trying to prepare you so you won't be surprised when you see her."

When they reached the room, Rebecca had tears in her eyes. Mary was the first to enter.

"Mother, I'm so glad you're all right," she said as they all gathered around the bed and took turns hugging and kissing her. She assured them she was doing just fine.

"I look a lot worse than I actually am," she said. "We don't have much time to be with one another before Dr. Gray sends you all away. I want all of you to listen to what I have to say. Ben, will you come here? Ben, these are our sons and daughters. Children, I want you to meet your Uncle Benjamin Davis. I know this is a surprise to you. I found out about Ben when I was in Chicago. I never knew I had a brother. There's something else I need to tell you before you leave. Aunt Lillian is our birth mother, Ben and I. It's a long story and I don't have time to explain everything right now, but please accept Ben as your uncle. In time, everything will be explained to you."

Sarah had been right. Her sons and daughters were surprised, actually shocked to hear what she had said. They had so many questions that needed to be answered, but they knew now was not the time to ask.

Dr. Gray asked them to leave for now, "You can visit her this afternoon after she is rested." They walked out of the room and went back to the waiting room. Ben and John followed behind them. Everyone was confused as to how all this had come about. Thomas waited for his father and Ben to catch up to him. He asked his father how long Ben had known about this.

"Thomas, I just found out your mother and I are sister and brother yesterday. I was told by my father and mother who adopted me when I was a young child. Before yesterday, I didn't even know I was adopted."

"We have thought that Aunt Lillian was our great-aunt. Now, mother tells us she's our grandmother," Rebecca said incredulously.

"Are you married, Uncle Ben?" Melanie asked him.

"Yes, I'm married. My wife's name is Beverly. We have a son and a daughter, Christopher and Catrina, and three grandchildren."

"Do you live in Detroit?" Robert asked him.

"No, I live in Atlanta. My father and mother live in Detroit."

"Who is your biological father?" Jimmie asked.

"From what I was told, Judge Ray Barnes is my father."

"Do you and mother have the same father?"

"I don't think we do, but I'm not sure at this point. There are a lot of things I don't understand myself. We all have a lot of questions to get answered," Ben said.

"Have you told your family about all of this?" John asked.

"Everything happened so fast, I didn't know what to tell them. My world has been turned upside down," he sighed as he held his head in his hands. "Before I tell my family, I need to handle all of this myself which is very difficult. I need to call Aunt Lillian and ask her some questions."

"You really mean your mother, don't you?" Rebecca reminded him.

"Yeah, I guess so. I guess I really have two mothers," Ben said. That did not sit well with him.

"What kind of doctor are you?" John Jr. asked him.

"I'm a doctor of internal medicine. I mostly do research on how to prevent and hopefully find a cure for the AIDS virus. I work for the Center for Disease Control in Atlanta. I was in Detroit for a conference when I met your mother. When I was informed about your mother being my sister, I didn't know what to do. I didn't want to come, but something inside made me. I feel like I lost my identity and my family when I was told about this. Since I've been here and met you as a family, I'm beginning to feel a little better, but I'm still conflicted. I have to be extremely careful not to alienate my mom and dad, though. How am I supposed to do all of this?" he asked.

"You do it very carefully, Ben, very carefully. This family has a lot of tenacity. We have always helped each other through the hard and difficult times. I know we have been brought together by strange circumstances, but everything will be all right. You'll see," John told him.

Ben picked up the phone and dialed Aunt Lillian's number. When she answered, he didn't know what to say.

"Hello?" she called.

He didn't say anything.

"Hello? Is anyone there?" she repeated.

He finally answered, "Hello, this is Ben."

"Oh, hi Ben," she answered. She could tell Ben was upset. She didn't blame him, given the circumstances. "Are you all right?" she asked.

"No," he replied. "I may never be all right again. If you're my mother, if you're really my mother, how could you have given your own flesh and blood away like I was some kind of meat you purchased from the supermarket? You let me be raised by two wonderful people that I have considered my biological parents which is great, but do you think just because you had a change of heart that you can come and destroy everyone's lives? If you're concerned today, why weren't you concerned when you gave me away? Just what do you think I should do with this information?"

"Ben, just what did your parents tell you?" she asked. She hadn't expected him to be happy, but she also hadn't expected such a venomous attack.

"They told me I was adopted when I was young and that you are my birth mother."

"Did they tell you why I gave you up for adoption?" she asked.

"They didn't go into why I was given up. They told me you would have to explain that to me. They were so upset they could barely manage to tell me about Sarah. They're so afraid they're going to lose me and my family. I'm afraid I might lose them also. Why did you have to make all of this known after being hidden for so many years?"

"You're right Ben. I never should have disturbed you and your parents. I should have carried all of these secrets with me to my grave. I would have if it hadn't been for your sister, Sarah. I'm not proud of what I've done to you and your family. Did your parents tell you who your father really is, or was?"

"They told me his name is Judge Ray Barnes."

"Do you know who he was?" she asked.

"No, not really. I have heard the name before, but I don't know who he is."

"He was a famous civil rights attorney and judge. The night you were conceived," she said as she took a deep breath, "he raped me. Sarah witnessed the whole thing. She's been plagued by nightmares most of her life. That is why she came to visit me. She was in search of answers that might help put an end to them. Ben, I hate to tell you this for I know, from experience, how much it must hurt. I thought, under the circumstances, the best thing to do was to give you up for adoption. Frank and Pat will always be your parents. I didn't do this for you to come running to me and forget about them. Sarah didn't know I was her mother until she came to visit. We started talking and all of this just came out. Once one of the secrets was out, all the rest came out too. Even if you and I never have any type of relationship, you and Sarah need to get to know each other as sister and brother. I really don't care about myself. I'm sorry that I caused you and your family so much pain." Aunt Lillian hung up without saying another word.

Ben stared at the phone as the busy signal sounded. All of this was so overwhelming. How in the world could he learn to cope when more and more secrets kept being thrown at him?

He decided to call his parents to let them know about Sarah's progress. His father answered the phone. He was surprised to hear Ben's voice.

"How are you, son?"

"I'm fine dad, how are you and mom?"

"We're okay, just thinking about you. How's Sarah?"

"She has regained consciousness. We visited with her for a while this morning. She's doing great."

"Have you met her family? I hear they're wonderful."

"I met them all. They're very nice people. Dad, this whole situation is very strange to me. I'm not going to let it change our relationship. You and mom are my parents and that's the way it's going to stay. Lillian may have brought me into this world, but you two are the ones who supported me all of my life," Ben said to his father.

"Ben, have you talked to Lillian? Did she explain the circumstances in which you were conceived?"

"Yes, she did."

"I'm not taking her side, but she went through a very difficult time. She was raped, her daughter witnessed it and was plagued with nightmares, and her husband left her because of it. She has had quite a lot to deal with. Maybe she thought she was doing the right thing for you at the time. We could always say what we would have done from where we are standing at the time, but hind sight is 20/20. Now we have the advantage of analyzing the whole situation and Lillian had to make a decision while still trying to deal with everything that was going on and live at the same time. If we were put into the situation not knowing what we know now, the decision would have been just as difficult for us. We might have made the same decision," Ben's father cautioned him. "Life isn't always cut and dry. Lord, we wish it was, but it's not. My mother used to tell me as a boy that your problems in life are like the birds. Sometimes, they will land in your tree but they won't remain there for long. They might seem as if they're there forever, but eventually they take flight and fly away. Ben, we've always loved you as our very own and that will never change. When we adopted you, we had tried to have children for five years. We learned that Pat couldn't carry to full term. We had thought about adoption and had talked with an adoption agency. We visited with some of the children that were up for adoption, but we never saw the one we wanted until we met you. You've brought so much joy into our lives. If we hadn't adopted you, we never would have known the joy of having a child. Son, try not to be so critical of Lillian. I'm sure she has entertained all the negative thoughts you could possibly send her way. We're here for you whenever you're ready to come home."

"Tell mother I love her very much," Ben said.

"I'll tell her, Ben. Take care of yourself and we'll talk again soon."

Ben hung up the receiver. He was trying to decide what to do next. He went back to the telephone and dialed Aunt Lillian's number again. This time when she answered, he said, "This is Ben."

"If you called to vent your criticism on me, I'm afraid I'm too tired to accommodate you, Ben."

"I'm trying to understand all this and I must admit I'm not doing very well at it. I don't mean to be rude to you. I guess I'm trying to sort things out before I tell my family this extraordinary story. Would you mind if I came to see you?" he asked.

"Are you sure you want to do that?" she countered.

"I know in order for us to get to know each other, we must be able to sit down and talk about the situation."

"Ben, you are welcome at my home anytime. Just let me know when to expect you," she said.

"I'll be there tomorrow."

Ben told John he was leaving for Chicago the next morning. "I'll return here the day after tomorrow. Tell Sarah I'm going to see Lillian. Tell her I'll be back." Then, he went to the waiting room to get his things.

"Are you leaving?" Thomas asked.

"Yes, I'm going to Chicago to see Lillian."

"Are you coming back?" Rebecca asked him.

"Yes, I'll be back the day after tomorrow."

"We've asked you a lot of questions about your family, but you know very little about ours," Mary noted.

"I have been around you long enough to know that what I have been told is true. There will be time for us to get to know one another. After all the questions are answered, hopefully we can come together as a family. Before I leave, I must tell you, your mother is one determined woman. If it had not been for her, we wouldn't have known each other. I'll continue to pray for her full recovery." Ben then left for his flight to Chicago.

DR. DAVIS VISITS AUNT LILLIAN

When Ben rang the doorbell, he didn't know what to expect from Lillian or from himself. He heard her coming to open the door, going through a number of locks before the door finally opened.

"Hi," she said. "How is Sarah doing?" she asked in an attempt to stay on neutral territory as long as possible.

"Sarah is doing fine. I spoke with her before leaving Knoxville. I feel like a fish out of water," he confessed as he followed her into the house.

"What do you mean?"

"There are so many questions I need for you to answer for me," he explained.

Lillian steadied herself. Although she had known this moment would come, she was still overcome with anxiety. Her heart raced as she asked what questions he had.

"Why did you give me away?"

"Ben," she sighed, "I didn't give you away. I let a couple, Mr. and Mrs. Davis, who had been unsuccessful in their attempts to have children, adopt you. I took time to choose the right home for you. It might not have been the right decision, but it was the only one I could make at the time."

"Did you ever regret it?"

"Ben," she said as she looked deep into his eyes, "I have lived to regret a lot of my decisions."

"How did Sarah react when she found out that you are her mother?"

"Sarah was astounded, just as you are. As one gets older, the things you could easily omit in your life become harder to reconcile. I was afraid that every time I looked at you, you would remind me of that awful night. I knew it was not your fault. You were a victim just like Sarah and me. I was afraid that if I didn't let someone adopt you, I might take my frustrations out on you. I couldn't let that happen, Ben."

"Did you love me?"

"No, not at first. I grew to love you. After I accepted the fact that I did nothing wrong to provoke the attack, I learned to love people again. It was not easy, but I eventually got past it. I always gave you a present on your birthday and at Christmas. I never wrote who it was from. I assumed you thought all of your presents came from Mr. and Mrs. Davis. I didn't want you to know anything about me."

"I think I remember seeing you at our house when I was very young," he said as he reminisced about his childhood. "I never thought much about it."

"You didn't have a reason to suspect anything. That is why I stopped coming to see you when I thought you were getting old enough to remember me," Aunt Lillian told him.

"Do you have any pictures of Sarah and me when we were born?"

"Yes, I do," she said as she moved to get them. "I'll be right back," she promised. Aunt Lillian disappeared down the hall in search of the photos. When she returned, she held a picture album full of photos of Ben and Sarah. She also had pictures of herself holding each of them when they were babies.

"Who is this?" he asked her as he focused on one of the pictures. "Is this you?" he asked as recognition dawned on his face.

"Yes," she said, smiling. "That picture was taken of me when I was 25 years old."

"You were a beautiful woman. Not that you aren't now."

"Oh, I know what you meant," she laughed. "I'm an old woman. Gravity has gotten a hold on me and won't let go." She smiled as Ben continued to look at the pictures. "Are you hungry?" she asked him.

"I guess I could eat something," he replied.

"I've been so preoccupied I've forgotten to eat," she said as she rose from the sofa. "Come, I'll fix you something."

"I don't want to trouble you," he said as he followed her out of the room.

"It's no trouble at all," she assured him. He followed her into the kitchen, noticing her every movement. He was trying to see what features he had that resembled her. As she fixed Ben something to eat, she asked him if he had ever made a mistake or made a decision he regretted later.

"Yes, I have, several times," he told her.

"In life, we have a lot of decisions to make. When I was a child, my grand-mother used to tell me that life is filled with decisions and choices that only you can make for yourself. Always try to make the correct one, she told me. But, if it turns out to be a bad one, try to correct it if you can. If you can't, just leave it alone and give it over to God," Aunt Lillian told him in an effort to make him understand her actions.

"Do you believe you made the best decision for all concerned when you decided to let mom and dad adopt me?"

"Yes, I do," she answered. "I believed then and I still believe today that I made the right decision for all concerned at that time. I knew when I made that decision that I could never change it." She finished preparing the food and asked Ben to sit at the table. She thanked the Lord for his mercy, kindness, and grace. "Oh, Lord," she prayed, "we thank you for the food that you have pro-vided for the nourishment of our bodies, Amen." They began eating together for the very first time.

"You're a Christian, aren't you?" Ben asked.

"Yes, I am," Aunt Lillian answered. "Do you and your family attend church?"

"Yes, we attend church on a regular basis. We all sing in different church choirs. Hmmmm" he groaned, "This food is delicious." He paused to savor the turkey club Aunt Lillian had prepared. "What kind of relationship do you sup-pose we're to have?"

"I really don't know," she answered. "I don't want you to hate me because of what happened. I will always love you and Sarah. I know I haven't been a mother to either of you. I don't require anything of you. I won't make any demands of you whatsoever. I don't want to interrupt your life any more than I have already. I would like for you and Sarah to get to know each other if you want to. I know she wants to very much. I don't believe she will impose on you and your family's privacy if you want things to remain the way they are now."

"I feel like my foundation has been ripped out from under me," he explained. "I do know I have to explain this to my family. I don't know how they are going to take it. If I tell them I was conceived during a rape, that might devastate them. Then again, they might understand better than I. There are so many people that I have to consider. The simple solution seems to be just to leave things as they are, but I realize the easy way isn't always the best way. At this point, I really don't know what to do," Ben said.

"I certainly don't know what to advise you to do," she responded as she pat-ted his hand.

"Maybe it's best if you don't mention this to your family just yet. If that's your decision,

Sarah and her family will have to understand."

"I don't know if I could live with myself if I decided not to tell them. I just don't know," Ben sighed. Just as he finished speaking, the phone rang. When Aunt Lillian answered, she was unable to catch the voice on the other end.

"Who is this, please?" she asked. She finally realized it was Sarah. "Sarah," she said, "oh baby, how are you doing?"

"I feel okay. John told me that Ben came to see you."

"Yes, he did. He's here now. Are you well enough to be talking on the phone?"

"The way I see it, it's just like talking with someone in the room with me. Dr. Gray didn't want me to, but I finally convinced him to let me make this one important call. Tell Ben I love him."

"Just one minute, Sarah. I'll let you tell him yourself," Aunt Lillian said and handed Ben the phone.

"Hello, Sarah."

"Hi. I'm so glad you went to see our mother. I know it's a strange visit, but as we get to know each other, it will get better. I just wanted to tell you that I love you and am looking forward to meeting your family. Oh, I'm afraid my time is up. I have to go, love you, hope to see you soon."

The phone call made Ben feel a little better. For the first time, he had a sister and she cared about him. It was a new feeling. It was ironic that she had called at the precise moment when he was wrestling with the decision of whether to tell his family.

"You know, Lill…, mother… I don't know what to call you," he said.

"Either one is just fine, Ben," she beamed, honored that he had even considered calling her mother.

"Sarah doesn't seem distraught by what has happened," he said.

"The most important thing to Sarah in life is her family," Aunt Lillian reflected. "Once she found out she had a brother, she kept asking questions until I told her your name and where you were. Family means everything to Sarah. If it had not been for her, I probably would never have revealed this to anyone."

"What happened to the man after he raped you?"

"You mean Ray Barnes?"

"Yes, that's who I mean," he said, being careful not to call him daddy or father.

"He became a very successful lawyer and judge. I received a letter from him when Sarah was here. I'll let you read it if you want to."

"Did you ever forgive him for what he did to you?"

"No, I never forgave him for violating all of us. The only good thing that came out of all of this was you, Ben. Would you like to read the letter he sent?" she asked, changing the subject. She didn't think she'd ever forgive Judge Barnes.

"If you don't mind, I would like to read it."

"I'll be right back," she said and went to go get the letter.

"There was no mention of me," Ben said after reading the letter. "Did he know he fathered a child when he raped you?"

"No, I never told him about my pregnancy. He never knew he had a son. I couldn't take the chance of putting your parents through a possible custody battle. At the time, I was sure that if I made it known, he might try to get you some way. Anyway, I didn't think he deserved to know. I felt like if I didn't send him to prison, we were even."

"It seems to me that he had a rough go of it himself," Ben responded. "Carrying around guilt can be worse than a prison sentence sometimes. I have had patients complaining about headaches and muscle spasms in the stomach and couldn't find anything wrong with them physically. Sometimes, these conditions are brought on by a guilt complex that triggers the nervous system in a negative way."

"He had a lot of success in the legal profession. If all of this is true, it would seem that he was miserable in his personal life, but he's the one who caused all of this," Aunt Lillian ground out. "We didn't ask for it. Maybe it was God's way of punishing him for all of the things he did to us."

"You still hate him for what he did to you, don't you?" he asked as he searched her face.

"Yes, I hate him. I know the Bible teaches forgiveness, but I'll never forgive him as long as I live."

"When you look at me, are you reminded of what happened?"

"I can't forget what happened, but I have learned to live with it," she answered. "I don't hate you, Ben. You are a part of me too. I love you and I love Sarah."

There was a moment of silence before she changed the subject. "Are you spending the night?"

"Well," he hedged, "I had planned on staying in a hotel."

"You don't have to do that. I have enough room for you. I would be honored if you stayed here," she said, hoping that he'd say yes. It was hard having him here, but it was nice also. She never thought she'd have her son in her home again.

"Well, if I'm not putting you out," he acquiesced, "I'll stay."

"Of course you're not putting me out. Let me show you to your room so you'll know where to put your things."

Ben followed Aunt Lillian out of the kitchen. As he walked through the violet-painted hallway, he was very aware of how uneasy he felt around Aunt Lillian. He was careful not to touch her or make contact with her in any way. He was afraid he would get emotionally tied to her. He wanted to maintain his close relationship with his parents which made this visit very hard on him. These recent events had exhausted him emotionally and physically.

"Lillian, do you mind if I take a short nap?"

"Of course not," she replied. She was so proud to have Ben in her home. She went over to the bed and turned back the cover as if she was getting ready to tuck him in. "If you need anything, just call. I'll be in the den watching my soaps," she said smiling.

"I'll be just fine. Thanks for everything," Ben told her as he moved to close the door behind her.

"You are welcome, Ben. I wish things had been different in our lives," she said wistfully as she headed toward the den.

He slept most of the afternoon. Aunt Lillian looked in occasionally to make sure he was all right. When he awoke, it took his eyes some time to adjust. As the room slowly came into focus, he looked around. The room was sparsely, but tastefully furnished. The walls had been painted a calming shade of blue. As was evidently her custom, the furniture was made out of dark, cherry wood and was designed with beautiful, but simple lines. As he pushed back the linen colored comforter, he swung his legs over the side of the bed using his feet to search for his shoes. He pulled himself off of the mattress and went in search of Aunt Lillian. She was laid back in her favorite recliner watching soap operas and snacking on some popcorn. She looked up as he walked into the room. As he sat down on the couch, he apologized for sleeping so long.

"You don't have to apologize for being tired," she said. "Seems to me like you needed that."

"I push myself pretty hard sometimes and the recent turn of events has compounded the stress."

"Your job sounds very rigorous," she replied.

"It can be. We have a lot of research to do and not enough time to do it. There is a rush to find a cure for the AIDS virus. We're competing with other countries although we share information with each other. Just like anything else, there is competition in the medical profession as well. The ultimate concern is to be able to eliminate this disease from society. In the search for the cure and to educate people on how to prevent themselves from contracting this deadly disease, my colleagues and I have traveled around the world."

Aunt Lillian gave him a nod of encouragement, seemingly very interested in his job. Ben continued, "In some of the third world countries, this disease is more deadly than any other. Most of the people are too poor to purchase condoms to use while having sex. Trying to tell them not to engage in sex without one is like telling them not to eat. In the really poor countries, that can be the only pleasure they get out of life. We've found several cases where the whole village is about 80% infected. Some of the countries have programs where the local government gives condoms to the people, but the resources that they have are very limited. Some of the people don't believe the threat is real so we have to try to overcome ignorance also. We have found that to be true in this country also. You would think that after all of the media exposure, especially here in the U.S., people would protect themselves by not having unprotected sex. We did a survey to determine if the advice was being followed. We were surprised to learn that there are a large number of people who think they can trust their partners and not practice safe sex. Some people think they can look at a person and determine if he or she has the AIDS virus. These people are putting their lives on the line," he said, shaking his head. It baffled him why people couldn't understand the reality surrounding them.

"I would think that with such a deadly disease, people would take it more seriously," Aunt Lillian replied, amazed that people could be so hard headed.

"Some people don't take it seriously at all. Illegal drugs have played a major role in developing this type of mind set among the public. Under the influence of mind-altering drugs, people are defenseless to take the proper steps to protect themselves. I'm afraid illegal drug use will be with us for a long time, in one form or another. We have a lot of social ills that are causing the populace to lower their defenses voluntarily and this is the type of environment that helps this disease perpetuate itself. I believe if we can educate the public about the correlation between illegal drug use and the AIDS virus, we'll be on our way to reducing the number of people infected by this deadly disease."

"I have heard a lot about the AIDS virus, but I never had the opportunity to talk with someone who is directly involved in searching for the cure. Your work is desperately needed. I know it must be frustrating at times to see people take this disease so lightly," Aunt Lillian replied.

"People need to remember this disease does not discriminate. It will infect anyone at any time regardless of color or social status. Everyone must take the proper precautions against it," Ben said as he averted his attention to the television, allowing himself to be distracted. He needed a break from talking about work.

"Have you talked with your family about going to Knoxville, Ben?" Aunt Lillian asked.

"I spoke with Beverly, but I didn't discuss the true nature of my trip. I told her it was a business meeting that I had to attend in Dr. Foster's place. I didn't want to confuse her about the situation. I need more time to analyze everything before I decide whether to tell her and the children about all of this," he explained. "I have to consider what impact this will have on them. If I decide not to tell them, I want you and Sarah to respect my decision and not pursue this any further. Right now, the only people involved on my side of the family are myself, mom, and dad. When I leave tomorrow, I might not ever see you again. It's not because I hate you or anything like that, but I think we might be too far along in life to try to heal old wounds. We might create new ones for other people in our lives. I don't believe that would be fair to them. I'm not saying that's going to be my decision. I just want to warn you of the possibility. I have been in the medical profession all of my life. My dad and mom taught me one valuable principle that has served me well. They taught me that if you can't make the patient's life better, try not to make it worse by the decisions you make. I must apply that same principle to this situation," he said.

"I understand your reasoning and I will respect your final decision, whatever it may be," she assured him. "I will do my best to accept it if it's to break contact with our side of the family. I'm glad you came to see me, Ben. This conversation is one that you and I needed to have in person. I have been concerned about your parents ever since Sarah and I visited with them. When they adopted you, I promised them that I would never reveal to you that I'm your birth mother. I broke that promise and I hope they'll forgive me. You have had a good life and you are doing good work trying to help humanity. Whatever you decide to do is your decision."

The next morning, Aunt Lillian prepared a light breakfast and went to Ben's room to wake him up. To her surprise, the room was empty. Ben had left during the night. There was a note on his pillow. It read:

I want to thank you for your hospitality. I couldn't sleep so I decided to leave for the airport. Besides, I'm not very good with good-byes. I don't know what we would have said to each other if I had stayed through the night anyway. I have come to believe that home is where the heart is and, right now, mine is with the parents I grew up with and with my wife and children.

'You could have stayed until morning. Instead, you slipped away in the middle of the night,' she thought as she brushed away a tear. 'Good-by Ben.'

Ben wanted to see Sarah before returning home. He stopped outside the airport. He dialed the number to the hospital and asked about Sarah's condition. He was told that she had improved and her condition had been upgraded to serious. He checked into the same hotel as before and waited a couple of hours before going to the hospital. Despite the note he'd left Aunt Lillian, he was still undecided as to what he would finally do. He knew he had to make a decision soon.

When he arrived at the hospital, he received a very warm greeting, unlike before. The difference was amazing and he laughed at the change. Ben asked to speak with John in private for a few minutes. He told John about his visit with Aunt Lillian.

"She's quite a lady, isn't she?" John asked.

"Yes, she is," Ben had to agree. Aunt Lillian had overcome a lot in her lifetime. "I know Sarah has her heart set on uniting all of us together as one happy family. I personally don't favor the idea. I have tried to convince myself by analyzing the situation, but I have concluded that it is not the right thing to do. I believe my family would be devastated to learn that I was conceived from the rape of a strange woman whom they know nothing about. I'm having a lot of problems with it myself. They have gone through life believing that my mom and dad are my real parents. All of our friends know them as my parents. They have attended our children's school functions and were there when they graduated from college. My colleagues know them as my parents. John, do you understand what I'm saying? As much as Sarah would like to make us one happy family, I think the consequences are too great. We'd end up creating deeper wounds for those we love and hold dear to our hearts."

"Ben, I understand how you feel," John said as he processed what Ben was telling him. Sarah was going to be very disappointed. "I respect your decision not to pursue this any further. I really don't know how we are going to tell Sarah. I'm worried about her health more than anything. If we tell her now, it might cause her condition to deteriorate. Are you going to see her before you leave tomorrow?"

"I don't think I will," Ben said, thinking of the magnitude of the situation. Once again, he was trapped in the middle. Every decision he made or didn't make seemed to effect those around him.

"I think you need to visit her before you leave," John suggested. "You don't have to tell her your decision, but I know she's looking forward to seeing you."

"If you insist," Ben reluctantly agreed.

He just wanted to get this visit over with and get back to his family. If seeing Sarah one more time before he left would make it easier, he'd do it.

"I'll see her before I leave, but only if you go with me."

"I'll be glad to," John agreed.

They walked toward Sarah's room in silence. When they got to her door, Ben paused for a moment before going in. Placing a hold on his emotions, he fixed a smile on his face and walked through the door.

Sarah's room was filled with flowers of all different colors. There were roses and lilies everywhere. Ben watched from the door as John approached Sarah's bed and told her that he had a surprise for her.

"What kind of surprise is it?" she asked as she eyed him suspiciously. At that moment, Ben entered the room and greeted her.

"Hello, Sarah," he said cheerfully. "How are you doing this evening?"

"I'm fine, Ben," she said excitedly. Her smile lit up her face. "How was your visit with Aunt Lillian? She's quite a lady, isn't she?"

"Yes, she is," he agreed for the second time that day. "I had an informative visit with her. I got answers to all the questions I asked her. Sarah, she thinks the world of you."

"She loves you too, Ben. Didn't she tell you?"

"Yes, we talked about that."

"We're planning a large Thanksgiving dinner at the farm this year and we want you to bring your family so everyone can meet," she invited. "Thanksgiving is an excellent time for family to get together. I'll need your address and telephone number so I can keep in touch with you and Beverly," she gushed.

"I will have to check with Beverly to see if she has made previous plans. I'll let you know," he stalled.

"Well, make sure you write down your number and address before you leave."

"I'll make sure I leave it with John," he promised. "Sarah, you're quite a woman. I wish you the best life has to offer. I wish things had been different when we were children. You would have been a great big sister," Ben said.

Sarah looked at him intently.

"That sounds like you're saying good-bye, Ben" she said.

"I guess I am for now. You continue to follow Dr. Gray's instructions and you'll be home before you know it. You and John have a wonderful family and I know you're proud of them," he said as he turned to leave. Ben was filled with so many mixed emotions. He knew deep down inside he was saying good-bye to Sarah for good. Before he left the room, Sarah called to him.

"Ben, I love you," she said. He looked her way, smiled, and continued out the door. John followed him out. Ben told him to tell Sarah that he was sorry for not telling her the truth.

"In a perfect world, none of this would have happened. Unfortunately, we don't live in a perfect world. John, I guess this is good-bye," he said as he shook John's hand. "I'll leave for home tomorrow on the early flight. Tell your family I'm glad to have met them." He turned and left the hospital.

John went back in to check on Sarah. She looked up as he entered the room.

"He's gone for good, isn't he?" she asked. John didn't want to tell her the truth, but he couldn't lie to her.

"Yes, he's gone," he told her. "I don't know if it's for good, only time will reveal that. Don't worry about it, Sarah. I want you to concentrate on getting well."

"It saddens me, John, but I'll be all right. I know he's doing what's best for his family. He might change his mind one day," she suggested. "I guess everything is so overwhelming for him. Did he give you his address and phone number?"

"No, he didn't. I really don't think he intended to."

"Maybe he'll surprise us and come to Thanksgiving dinner," she said. At his pointed look, she shrugged her shoulders and said, "Well, I can hope, can't I?"

"In this world, hope is all we have sometimes," John reflected.

"I'll be glad to get home, John," she responded. "It seems as if I've been away for an awfully long time."

"I think it's because of the trauma you've been through," he said. "I felt the same way when I was in the hospital. I'll talk to Dr. Gray and see when he thinks you will be well enough to leave here."

"Has Aunt Lillian called since Ben returned?" she asked, worried about how her mother was taking all this.

"I haven't heard from her," he said. "Maybe I should call and see if she's okay," he said as he got up.

"That's a good idea," she agreed "I don't think Dr. Gray will let me have another phone in here. Tell her I'll call her as soon as I can. Tell her Ben will leave for home tomorrow morning."

"I'll tell her," he promised and kissed her on the cheek. "I'm going to leave you alone now so you can get some rest."

When John left the room, Sarah allowed the tears to flow. Unchecked, they didn't stop until they landed on her pillow. "Oh, Ben," she sighed as the tears continued to fall.

John was there the next morning when Dr. Gray was making his rounds.

"When do you think Sarah will be well enough to go home?" he asked the doctor.

"Sarah is progressing very well. I'm personally satisfied with her progress. Today, I'll examine her completely and, if everything goes well, I'll take the remaining bandages off her face tomorrow. There will be a few scars that might or might not need plastic surgery. They're closed and healing nicely. Let me answer your question tomorrow morning after I have all of the information that I need," Dr. Gray told him.

"That'll be just fine," John said, pleased with the doctor's response. "I need to make some arrangements so I'll be ready to take her home once she's released."

"Oh, by the way Mr. Goodwin, have you seen Dr. Davis?"

"Yes, he left for home this morning. I don't think he'll be coming back."

"I enjoyed talking with him. Please, give him my regards when you see him," Dr. Gray said as he continued on his rounds.

John called Aunt Lillian before going to see Sarah. When she answered the phone, she didn't seem to be herself. She was withdrawn and quiet. She told John to tell Sarah to just let things be.

"Tell her I'm praying for her and I'm looking forward to being with her and the family on Thanksgiving Day," she said.

"I'll tell her, Aunt Lillian," he promised. "I believe she will be released soon. I think she's getting tired of the hospital."

"Well, John, it doesn't take long for you to get tired of those hospitals. I'm not proud of what I've done concerning her and Ben. I believe I made the best decision I could have made at the time. I feel like I've made such a mess of everything. I just don't know what to do."

"Aunt Lillian, you can't keep punishing yourself for decisions that were made long ago. God has forgiven you. Now, you have to forgive yourself and go on with your life. If you make yourself sick over this, it's not going to change anything. It's easy for someone to say what he or she would do in any given situation, but one never knows until he or she is put into that situation. You made the best decision you could."

"Thanks, John. I'm going to take your advice. Tell Sarah I love her."

"She told me to tell you she will call you as soon as she can. Dr. Gray won't let her have another phone in her room. I'm going to tell you this and I'm going to let you go. Ben left for home today."

"I hope he finds his family in good spirits. Tell the family I will be there for Thanksgiving. I'll talk with you later, John. Good-bye."

SARAH IS DISCHARGED FROM THE HOSPITAL

Two days later, Sarah was released from the hospital. John had reserved a conversion van to take her home. He was not about to let her get on another airplane. Dr. Gray told John to notify Sarah's doctor of what had happened as soon as they got home. He asked John to drive safely and to take his time.

"You should stop periodically so she can walk around. Instead of driving straight through, you should consider staying overnight in Atlanta. That way the trip won't be too much for her."

"Dr. Gray, I will take your advice," John said.

"Does the van have a bed in it?" he asked.

"Yes, it does," John said.

"Good, if she starts to feel fatigued make sure she lies down. That will help to relieve it. If you need me, these are my numbers," he said as he handed John a slip of paper. "You should be able to reach me at one of them. Good luck, Mr. and Mrs. Goodwin. I hope you have a safe journey home."

Before leaving, Sarah and her family thanked the hospital staff. She told them that if they were ever in Georgia to give her a call. They said their good-byes and went on their way. Sarah was glad to be leaving the hospital.

John Jr. was in charge of the driving. They stopped several times before arriving in Atlanta where they spent the night.

When they arrived at the hotel, John requested a room on the ground floor so Sarah would have easy access to and from the van. There was a restaurant located on the ground floor of the hotel and John was suddenly reminded of how long it had been since they'd eaten. He asked Sarah if she wanted him to get her some dinner before she went to bed. She told John that she wanted to go to the restaurant with him. She assured him that she felt like going so he took her hand and they walked there. Some people stared at the visible scars on her face and probably wondered what had happened to her, but Sarah didn't let it bother her. She enjoyed the meal with her family.

Before turning in for the night, she looked in the telephone directory for Dr. Benjamin Davis' number and address. She knew it was a long shot. It wasn't common for doctors to have their home numbers listed in the phone book, but she looked anyway. To her delight, Dr. Benjamin Davis was listed. She wrote down the number on a piece of paper and put it in her purse. She was careful not to let John see her.

The next morning after breakfast, they loaded the van and started for home. Sarah had enjoyed a restful night and had a little pep in her step. She told John again that she would be glad to get home. They arrived about three and a half hours later. John opened the door for her and went back to the van to help with the luggage. Sarah made her way into their home to her favorite chair and sat down.

"I'm home at last," she said. "There were times I thought I'd never see this place again." Charlie had done such a wonderful job taking care of everything. After they had settled in, John called Sarah's doctors to make an appointment. He explained to the nurses what had happened and that Sarah was one of the passengers who survived flight #526. That really got the nurse's attention. She told John to bring Sarah in the following day at 10 a.m.

When Sarah arrived at the doctor's office, there were photographers waiting to take pictures of her. The nurse had told some people who were in the office at the time John called and word got around fast. Everyone in the city of Ellaville knew John and Sarah. They had lived there practically their whole lives. The town was treating Sarah like a celebrity. She was told that it's not often that you meet someone who survived an airplane crash. Some people were even asking for her photograph.

John and Sarah were amazed at the reception they received in front of the doctor's office. There were hundreds of people who came to see "the lady who survived the plane crash." It would have been a big deal anywhere, but in a small place like Ellaville, it was overwhelming. Everywhere they went, it was the talk of the town. A couple of weeks later, the town showed how much they cared by proclaiming a Sarah Goodwin Day. Sarah Goodwin had done some-thing no other person in the history of the town had done. By surviving the crash, she brought national attention to Ellaville, GA.

The week of Thanksgiving, the Goodwin's were excited about the family getting together. Thanksgiving was John and Sarah's favorite time of the year, a special time for the family to come together and give thanks to God. John was busy around the farm, preparing for the arrival of his family.

Aunt Lillian arrived on Tuesday, by train. She told John and Sarah she would never travel by plane again. Their children started arriving on Wednesday and were all there by Thursday morning. Their home was filled with laughter as their grandchildren ran around looking at animals. John's grandchildren asked if he could take them fishing at the pond before they had to go home. The pond had always been one of their favorite places on the farm. John assured them they were going to go fishing on Friday morning. He and his family were really having a great time.

In line with tradition, most of the food was prepared on Wednesday. There was so much activity around the house. It was exciting just to be around it.

On Thursday morning, everyone had a light breakfast. They were saving themselves for the Thanksgiving feast. John and the men of the family arranged the tables and chairs in the backyard. The weather was so pleasant they had decided to have dinner outside this year. While the women made the final preparations to bring the food, John and his sons discussed future plans for the farm. They talked about their original suggestion of finding a young couple who would be interested in entering into a partnership.

Sarah interrupted the conversation to ask if the tables were ready.

"They're as ready as they'll ever be," John teased her. After promising his sons that they would finish their conversation later, he pitched in and helped her and the women bring the food from the kitchen and place it on the tables. When they finished, they all gathered around the table and stood behind their chairs. John had carefully counted everyone and made sure he placed enough chairs at the tables, but before the prayer, Sarah asked John to place four more chairs at their table.

"Honey, I counted to make sure. We have enough," he told her.

"Please, place four more, John," she insisted. Confused, but cooperative, John Jr. and Robert said they would get them. They just wanted their mom to be happy. After they had done what she requested, John asked everyone to hold hands as he said a prayer and blessed the food.

THE THANKSGIVING
PRAYER

John started his prayer by saying, "Our Heavenly Father, we acknowledge you in all that we do. We give you all the honor and glory for sharing life itself with us. We give thanks to you for allowing us to gather here today, for the safe journey of our family, who is here to celebrate and praise, in your mighty name, for all that we have. We realize you have all power in your hands. This farm, this Earth, this universe, and the fullness thereof, is yours, Holy Father. Help us to be aware, all the days of our lives, that we are a part of your family and we share in the richness thereof. We're your children and you're our Heavenly Father. We're like lost sheep, not knowing which way to go. Christ Jesus, you're the Good Shepherd who always leads us into greener pastures. You're the provider and you select the channel in which all of your blessings flow. Continue to help us to be good stewards while we're here on Earth. Father, we thank you for your compassion, your knowledge, your wisdom, and your understanding that you share with us in our everyday lives. We give thanks to you, Christ Jesus, for the shedding of your blood for the remission of our sins. Help us to keep our spiritual ears open and in tune with you so we can hear and obey when you speak. When we're in difficulty, help us to be patient, to pray, and wait on you. So, when testing times come, we will be able to stand firm because you are standing with us. We thank you for the favor that you have placed upon this family for we know we have come this far because of your grace. Help us continue to discern the difference between earthly wealth and the richness of your kingdom. We understand that the wealth of this world belongs to you and you alone and that you only share it with us while the spirit of life that you gave us expresses itself through us. The richness of your kingdom, that we can attain through the teachings and the examples that you shared with us when you were here on Earth, will be with us throughout eternity as we return home to be with you and our Heavenly Family, which is the richest family on earth as it is in heaven. Father, we worship and praise your mighty name and ask you to grant us these blessings in Christ Jesus' name. Amen."

When he finished, they sat down to a Thanksgiving dinner that was worthy of kings and queens. Nicolas, their grandson, asked Sarah who the four empty chairs were for.

"They are for members of the family that you have not met," she explained.

"Are they coming?" he asked, wondering why they were so late.

"I don't think so," she said.

"Then why did you have the chairs put there?" he asked, confused.

"When those four empty chairs are filled, it will make our family complete."

"Grandma," he said as he reached for her hand, "maybe they will come next year."

"Yes, Nicolas, maybe they will come next year," she agreed as she affectionately squeezed his hand.

The four empty chairs were a reminder to Sarah of her brother Ben and his wife and family. She had no way of knowing if they would ever be filled by them, but she was hopeful that someday they would. Today, she was content to be joyful. She had a lot to be thankful for on this Thanksgiving Day.

978-0-595-34035-4
0-595-34035-0